Looking for Art
Bert Robbens

Copyright © 2013

CHAPTER 1

It was February. Snowplows, shovels, and salt had reduced the last snowstorm to a ridge of greasy gray ice and slush mounded over the curbs of Davis Square. Ignoring the don't walk signal, Joe Polito spotted a break in the traffic, stepped over the mound of slush, and ran across Highland, one of the main streets coming into the square. Polito was a little less than average height, thick and solid from his ankles to his neck. He was in his early forties, but he moved with the quickness of a running back. He carried a paperback book and wore sneakers, jeans and a hooded sweatshirt. When he rounded the corner and went into the Old Town Tavern, he flipped the hood down as the only acknowledgement of the temperature difference between inside and outside. He had dark hair and a broad forehead that tapered down to a square jaw. Except for the book, he looked like the kind of guy you'd see standing on the sidewalk in front of the bar, smoking a cigarette and scaring the college girls and Yuppies who were taking over the square.

The Old Town Tavern had been a fixture in Somerville for more than fifty years. The building had been there for a hundred. Most of the interior hadn't changed. The dark wood floor was original, as was the stamped tin ceiling. The bar was heavy wood, inlaid with some kind of textured black plastic. It had probably been installed when the tavern had taken over the space. It was all good material and workmanship, but it had seen a lot of service. The Yuppies would have taken over the place and called it "shabby chic" if they hadn't been stiff-armed by the townies who considered it their turf.

It was just after noon on a Wednesday. There were only two other guys in the place. As Polito walked past the bar, he asked Tim, the bartender, to bring him his lunch at the usual table in back.

An hour later, a slender, dark haired woman of about the same age as Polito entered the bar. She wore a black wool, knee-length coat and low heels. She stopped just inside the door and scanned the room once, very deliberately. When she spotted Polito at his table in the back, she walked toward him, heels tapping the floor in a tight, even rhythm. The men watched her with undisguised curiosity. She was the kind of woman who would leave her Lexus double-parked and running on Elm Street while she went in to pick up her dry cleaning. She was not the kind who came into the Old Town Tavern on a Wednesday afternoon.

Polito put down his book and watched her approach, his face expressionless. When she stood before him, she said in a cool, polite voice without any Boston accent: "Mr. Polito, my name is Eileen Merrill. I wonder if you'd have a moment to talk to me."

"Yeah, sure," he said. Polito's accent was thick. He sat up a little straighter. "Have a seat."

"Thank you." She unbuttoned her coat and sat down. Beneath the coat she wore a gray business suit with a white blouse.

Polito glanced around at Tim and the men at the bar, who quickly looked away. When he looked back, she seemed to be going over him as if he was a new car she was thinking of buying. He should have resented it, but his normal reactions got shoved aside by curiosity and male deference to an attractive woman.

"You want anything?" he asked, nodding at the remains of a ham sandwich and a beer that sat on the table.

"No. No thank you. I've had my lunch."

She had an oval face with a rounded jaw and clear pale skin, a narrow nose with slightly flaring nostrils and thick brown hair that curled softly at her shoulder. There was an unusual poise in the carriage of her back and shoulders that was softened by the candor in her eyes, eyes that said she was all there, nothing held back.

"I think you know my father," she said, "Art Delaney."

Polito nodded. "Yeah, yeah. I know Art. Haven't seen him in a couple weeks, but he's a regular."

"That's what I wanted to talk to you about. I haven't seen him or heard from him either, not since a week ago last Thursday. I think something has happened to him, and I need help finding him."

"And you think I can help?" Polito frowned. "Why me?"

"My father told me some … things about you. One of his friends said you've helped other people with similar problems."

"Who was that?"

"Tommy Ahearn."

Polito made a sour face. "Oh, Jesus."

Her eyes clouded and her forehead furrowed. "Was he wrong?"

"He must think I'm in business or something. I do him a favor and now he's trying to sell me everywhere he goes."

"I see," she said, still with the worried look. "So, you're not in business?"

"No. If I help people out it's because they're my friends and they need help and it's something I can do."

"I'm sorry. I must have misunderstood what Mr. Ahearn was saying. I was hoping I could hire you to help me find my father." Some of the starch seemed to go out of her.

"What about the police?" Polito suggested.

"I've talked to them. They don't seem very interested. You're probably aware of my father's past."

"True. I guess they wouldn't be jumping through any hoops for him."

"No." She shook her head grimly. "They're not jumping through any hoops."

"But what makes you think I could find him?"

Because you know him. You know his friends. You know where he hangs out. You wouldn't be starting from scratch. And besides ..." Her eyes drifted away, as if she was afraid she might go too far.

"What?"

"It's just that some of the things I heard about you made me think you might have some ... special abilities for this kind of thing."

"What'd you hear?"

"That you were a cop." Her eyes came back to lock onto his, steady and clear. "That you got kicked off the force for reasons that were questionable. That you've still got friends in the Somerville PD, but you keep in touch with the tough guys, too. You're not one of them, but they think you're a 'stand-up guy' just the same."

"Art said all this?"

"And Tommy."

"And you bought it?"

"I didn't say that." She shook her head and smiled, but there was a shadow of sadness in it. "It sounded good enough to be worth checking out."

Polito smiled back. "So what do you think now?"

"I think there might be an ounce of truth in it."

"That's about right – an ounce of truth in a pound of bullshit."

"That's not a bad ratio." She said it casually, smiling, but her eyes were fixed on his.

"Maybe not," he shrugged.

"And now I'm really sorry you're not available."

"I didn't say that. I just said I wouldn't do it for money. I help my friends."

She didn't say anything, just waited, watching him.

"Art's a friend," he muttered, embarrassed and angry with himself. "I'll ask around. I know some of his friends. Maybe somebody heard something."

"Thank you," she said warmly, then got right back to business. "I know you don't want money, but it might help with some of Art's friends – something to get them talking."

"Yeah, it might."

She started to reach for her purse.

"Not here," Polito said without looking around. "These guys don't need to know about you."

"Oh. Yes. Of course."

"Who else have you talked to?"

"Just Tommy."

"Good. Let's get out of here."

Polito stuffed his book into the pocket of his sweatshirt and they walked out to the street. The men watched them all the way to the door. Outside, Polito checked up and down the street, didn't see anyone he knew.

He said, "How'd you get here?"

"By car. I'm parked in the lot around the corner."

"Okay, I'll walk you to your car. Tell me what you know."

They walked along Elm Street away from the square, past the dollar store, the McDonalds, the used CD store, the meat market, and the Tibetan restaurant. The common wisdom was that Davis would be the next Harvard Square, its upscale neighbor two stops inbound on the Red Line. Davis Square still had a long way to go, but the process had started. Rents were going up. More and more of the new businesses catered to the cosmopolitan, high-fashion, high-price tastes of the Yuppies. Joe Polito had lived within half a mile of the square his entire life, but he was starting to feel like an outsider. Eileen Merrill looked like she could belong anywhere. Her gaze took in the gritty street without comment, and her heels negotiated the uneven brick sidewalks with the assurance of a cat.

"I talked to Art on the phone two weeks ago tomorrow," she said. "I haven't heard from him since. I tried calling him several times - no answer. Two days ago, I went to his apartment. I have a key. There didn't seem to be anything out of place, except his mail had piled up and he wasn't there. That's when I called the police. Yesterday, I went down to the station and filled out a form. I got the distinct impression the form would sit on somebody's desk until they had nothing else to do, which might never happen. That's when I called Tommy. He didn't know anything, either, but he suggested you."

"Art never said anything about going away, something he was going to do, anything?"

"No. I keep trying to remember. I can't think of anything. And he would have told us. He's very close to his grandson."

"Did he need money?"

"Not that I know of. If he did, I would have been glad to give him some, but he'd never take it from me. He always said he wanted to do something for me, not the other way around."

"So maybe he wanted to get his hands on some money, for you."

"I doubt it. I don't need it, and he's been saying that ever since my mother divorced him. You know Art. He means well, but it's mostly talk."

"True."

They turned the corner and crossed to the parking lot. She pushed a button on her clicker and got in her car. She sat in the driver's seat with the door open and rummaged in her purse, pulling out some bills. "Is this enough?" she asked, handing them to Polito.

"Plenty, but I'd like the key to Art's place, too. And write down his address and your phone number."

She took a business card out of her wallet and scribbled some numbers. She handed him the card and the key, and took his hands in hers. He noticed the warmth and softness of her hands.

"I don't know how to thank you," she said. In the daylight, her eyes were lighter, an indeterminate shade of gray, almost green. "I couldn't just let it go. Art's never been the greatest father, but since my mother died, he's all I've got, and he means the world to Jake. I'd be at a dead end without you."

"No problem. I'll call you."

"Thanks." The speculative look scanned him again as she backed out of the space and drove away. Her business card said Eileen Merrill, Vice President and Legal Counsel, Netwave Technologies. Her car was a shiny black, nearly new, Lexus SUV.

CHAPTER 2

Polito didn't go back to the bar. Instead he turned away from the square, headed toward the address Eileen Merrill had given him for Art's place. It was only a few blocks away.

Eileen Merrill bothered him. He felt an unreasoning anger toward her as a type and a perverse attraction to her as an individual. In general, and below the level of consciousness, he held her breed of upper-middle class, aggressive, professional women responsible for many of the social slights that his class of blue-collar, underachieving, ambitionless men endured. She was part of everything that was wrong with the world. But when she walked into his tavern, his turf, and he let her take over like he had nothing better to do, he was worse; he was pathetic. She was beautiful and provocative. She knew it and used it, and he fell for it like an eager puppy. His head churned through the contradictions, and he cursed himself for a fool.

He crossed a side street against the light, oblivious to his surroundings. A BMW started to turn the corner and had to wait for him. The driver gave him a couple blasts of his horn. Polito stopped in the middle of the crosswalk, right in front of him, and gave him the finger. His harsh and eager smile should have warned the driver, but it didn't.

The guy rolled down his window. He was wearing a sweater over a dress shirt and tie. "You got something to say to me," he yelled.

"Lay off the horn, asshole," Polito yelled back.

The driver opened his door as if he was about to get out. "You want to come over here and say that?"

"Yeah." Polito smiled and walked around to his door. Very clearly, emphasizing each word, he said, "I said, lay off the fucking horn, asshole."

At that point, the driver was stuck. He didn't like it, but he got out of the car. "Fuck you," he said without conviction.

He was younger than Polito, about thirty, with brown wavy hair in a long layered cut, and he was tan, in late February, in Boston. At six-two and trim from work-outs at the gym, he looked like a good match for Polito, who was four inches shorter but outweighed him by a few pounds.

"You want to do something about it," Polito said, pushing a finger into his chest.

He swatted Polito's hand away and tried to push him with both hands. For Polito, that was invitation enough. He blocked the hands off to the side and the driver stumbled forward. Before he could get his balance, Polito brought a left hook around to his chin. There was a satisfying crack and the guy went down like he'd been shot.

Polito stood over him as he lay motionless for a ten count. When he started to moan and brought his hand to his face, Polito turned and went unhurriedly on his way, leaving the young man lying next to his car in the middle of the intersection. A few cars started to pile up behind him. One of them honked. When Polito was halfway down the block, he looked back and saw a couple college kids helping the BMW driver to his feet.

Polito knew it was stupid, but he couldn't help it. If it happened again, he knew he'd do the same thing. It was in his blood.

CHAPTER 3

Art Delaney's place was on a little side street called Elston just a few blocks from the square. Polito knew the street. He'd played on it when he was a kid, but he hadn't seen it in a few years. He was surprised at how prosperous it looked. The houses were mostly modest two-families, many sided with vinyl. But the tiny front yards were neat and nearly all the houses showed evidence of recent renovation and upkeep. It wasn't "Slummerville" anymore. Houses that might have sold for $30,000 in the early seventies were going for hundreds of thousands, half a million, or more. It meant that streets like Elston, shabby and decaying twenty years before, were now well-kept and appealing. It meant money in the pockets of the old-time Somervillains, too, but it was doing what 40 years of blight couldn't. It was moving them out. As far as Polito was concerned, that was a trade-off that wasn't worth it. He didn't like the people who were moving in.

One of the few houses on the street that had not yet been reclaimed was a vinyl-sided two-family that matched the address on the back of Eileen Merrill's card. The wooden porch sagged and needed paint. The tiny yard in front was overgrown with weeds and trash, and the veneer on the front door was scabbed and peeling around the edges. There were two cars in the narrow driveway, a 10 year old Ford boxed in behind a newer Toyota.

On the front porch, three metal mailboxes hung on the wall next to the door. One of them said Delaney, #3. Polito didn't need a key to get in. The front door had sagged and swollen too much to close properly. He pushed it open and walked into a dark, carpeted foyer that smelled of garlic and rotting wood. The odor followed him to the third floor. He knocked before he used the key and went in.

There wasn't much to the apartment. It was a converted attic from a time when the city had turned a blind eye to the zoning and building code violations of such unofficial residences. It had a kitchen and bathroom in the back and a single room in front for living and sleeping. Polito walked through quickly to see if anything jumped out at him. It didn't.

The ceilings were low and sloped where the roof cut in on both sides. There were two windows, side-by-side in front, looking down on the street. Two matching windows in the kitchen looked down on backyards clogged with fences, trash cans, piles of dead leaves and dirty slush. Outside, it was a nice winter day, with patches of blue sky showing through the clouds, a light breeze, around 40 degrees. But Art's place was collecting all the heat that rose from the two apartments below. It was stuffy, with the building's characteristic scent pervading. Polito cracked a window in front and one in back to get some air moving through.

The place was surprisingly clean, no dirty dishes in the sink or on the kitchen counter. The garbage can was only half full, mostly cardboard and plastic packaging from frozen dinners. Half a quart of milk had gone sour in the small and ancient refrigerator. Polito poured it down the sink and ran the tap. Besides the milk, there was some cheese, a jar of pickles, and two cans of beer in the refrigerator. In the cupboards, along with a couple cans of soup and a jar of instant coffee, there were individual plastic containers of jelly and paper packets of sugar, salt and pepper that Art must have pilfered from a restaurant. There wasn't much, but what there was was in its place, neat and clean.

The only clutter in the kitchen was a stack of junk mail on the counter. Polito sifted through it without much interest. There were a dozen credit card offers from major financial institutions. Polito couldn't see why they were so eager to give credit to an ex-con with no job and no assets, but that was their problem. Then there were another dozen that were obvious requests for some kind of charitable contribution. Good luck to them. Another waste of paper and postage, he thought. Then one of them caught his eye. It was from an organization called United Catholic Missions and the address was specific to Mr. Arthur Delaney. It didn't quite look like a mass mailing. He ripped it open and read the brief letter inside.

Dear Mr. Delaney,

Thank you for your interest in our saving work. As you know, we are entirely dependent upon the generous support of concerned Catholics like you who truly understand Christ's call to help the sick and poor, as we spread his message of love and redemption to all who will hear. We currently support Catholic missions in 17 countries where the need for spiritual and material assistance is most urgent. Unfortunately, due to the limitations of current funding, we are unable to support any further expansion of our missions at this time. We will keep your inquiry on file with the hope that future funding will allow us to add committed missionary hands and hearts such as yours to meet the ever growing needs of this troubled world.

Please help us meet those needs now with a donation (donation card and prepaid mailer enclosed). It is one more critically important way to further Our Savior's mission on earth. God be with you.

David Costello
United Catholic Missions

He folded the letter, put it in his pocket, and went out to the living/bedroom. It was just as neat as the kitchen. In the corner, an easy chair faced a small TV on a metal stand. A low table sat next to the chair. The only thing on the table was a small ceramic ashtray. Even that was neat, no ashes, no butts. A small bureau stood in the other corner under an ornate mirror. The bed was a mattress and box spring in an old brass frame. It was covered with a brown cotton spread, neatly tucked in around the pillows. The only thing out of place in the whole room was a red and blue striped tie folded once and laid out neatly on the bed. Polito went through the drawers and closet, pausing now and then to examine one or another of Delaney's meager possessions. The closet contained all of his pants, shirts, shoes, coats and hats. The clothes were all cheap, rough and worn. It was a small closet, but Art's things didn't even fill it. When Polito kicked around a couple pairs of shoes arranged neatly on the floor, he noticed something he couldn't immediately place, something inside one of the shoes. He picked it up and pulled out a neatly rolled bundle of hundred dollar bills held together with a rubber band. He fanned through the bills and determined they were all $100s, no $1s, no paper inserts, around 100 of them he guessed - $10,000. He put the bundle in his pants pocket, where it made a bulge, but the color of the money was hidden.

He looked around for a few more minutes. In the bathroom, he found soap, toilet paper, a few towels and some over-the-counter medications – foot cream, eye drops, antacids. There was no toothbrush or razor.

Joe took a final look around and closed up the apartment. As he was going down the stairs, he heard a woman coming up, evidently heading for the second floor apartment. Polito stopped on the landing to let her pass.

She was average height and skinny. Frowsy bleached blonde hair was gathered loosely in a bun at the back of her head, and she was smoking a cigarette. She wore a black car coat over green scrubs and sneakers and had the cigarette stuck between her lips as she dug through a huge black purse, evidently looking for her keys.

"Excuse me," Polito said. "I was looking for Mr. Delaney upstairs. I guess he's not home. Any idea where I might find him?"

She stopped on the last step and looked up, startled. A frown of suspicion quickly resolved into a more hopeful look of interest as she stepped up to the landing and looked him over, squinting to keep the smoke out of her eyes. "Who're you?"

"My name's Joe Polito. Art's daughter asked me to check up on him, said she hadn't heard from him for a few days."

She found the keys, but didn't use them. "Hasn't been here for days," she shrugged. "I got no idea where he is."

"You remember when the last time you saw him was?"

"I don't know – a few weeks ago maybe, but I heard him about a week ago. Woke me up in the middle of the night. Sounded like a goddamn herd of elephants going up these friggin' stairs. Every step, cracking and squeaking like the whole damn building's going down."

She was approaching 40, but the years had been hard ones. Her face was puffy and cracked under blotchy make up, and the hair looked brittle enough to be swept away with a good brushing. She took the cigarette out of her lips and smiled. "Old man Greavey – he owns the place - I told him he ought to do some repairs. It'd be worth it. A house down the street just like this one went for over 600K last summer."

"I believe it. But, Delaney – when was that time you heard him going up the stairs?"

"I don't know. Let me think." The smile turned coy. "Listen, you want to come in for a cup of coffee? I just got off shift and I'm dead on my feet."

"Sure, why not." Polito smiled back.

She unlocked the door and they filed into a narrow hall. "Don't look at the place. It's a mess. I've been taking extra shifts on weekends, so I never get any time for cleaning."

They walked into the kitchen and Polito saw she wasn't kidding. Every plate, dish, glass, pot, pan, knife and fork she owned was piled around the sink and crusted with food. Old newspapers and magazines were tossed haphazardly in a corner next to a black plastic garbage bag that was full of something. On a small Formica table there was nothing but an overflowing ashtray and a mug of coffee dregs. Matching chairs of pitted chrome and red plastic upholstery stood on each side of the table.

"Grab a seat," she said, throwing her purse on the last vacant space on the counter and opening a refrigerator that was the twin of the one upstairs. "How about a beer instead of coffee? That's what I'm having."

"Even better." Polito smiled encouragement and pulled out one of the chairs.

She put two cans of Bud Light on the table and dropped heavily onto the other chair. "Oh, god. That's better," she sighed. "I must walk twenty miles in a shift, I swear to god."

"What do you do?"

"Work at Somerville Hospital, nurse's aide. You might not think that's so tough, but you're on your feet all day. If I get to sit down 20 minutes in a shift, that's a good day."

"Must drive you crazy when Delaney wakes you up."

"No shit. I got to be up at six every morning. My name's Lisa Landry, by the way. Nice to meet you, Joe." She stuck out her hand and Polito shook it.

"You too."

She took a long pull from the can and leaned back with a sigh. "Now that I think about it, I remember when the old man woke me up. It was a week ago last Saturday. I remember because I went out that night, got in late, even though I had to work the next morning. Then Delaney comes in – must have been three in the morning – sounds like all the souls in hell marching up the stairs."

"Somebody with him?"

18

She made an exaggerated shrug. "Who knows. The noise those stairs make, one person sounds like an army. T'tell you the truth, I was half in the bag."

She brought the can to her lips and tilted it up while her throat chugged down the other half of the can. Her eyes were momentarily bright when she brought the empty can down on the table with a sharp click. "Ah, nothing like that first beer of the day. Except maybe the second. You want another."

"Oh, no thanks. I've got to be going."

Lisa made a disappointed pout. "You going to leave me to drink all alone? I thought maybe we could have a little party, you know?"

"Any other time I'd like to, but I'm supposed to meet a friend of mine in Davis. He's going to be wondering where the hell I am."

She went to the refrigerator and got another can of beer. She cocked a hip and leaned against the counter, smiling at him with half-closed eyes. "Let him wait. We got more important things to do right here."

Polito drained his can and stood up. "Can't right now."

He took two steps and stood before her. She looked up at him with mild speculation. Joe put his hands on her hips and pulled her to him.

"I want you to know I appreciate the offer," he said and kissed her.

She responded eagerly, putting her arms around him and grinding her pelvis against his. Her mouth opened softly to his. But Joe pulled away.

"Got to go," he whispered.

"No," she moaned.

"Got to." He smiled and left.

CHAPTER 4

Not much had changed when Polito got back to the Tavern. It was mid-afternoon and there were half a dozen guys at the bar and three more at a table. Polito got a beer at the bar and took it to his table. He pulled his book out of the pouch of his sweatshirt and sat down to read.

He didn't get to read much. Ten minutes later Paul Shea came in. Paul was a Somerville cop, about the same age as Polito, but taller and wiry. He carried his uniform cap in his hand, as if he was in a church or hoped to hide his official function. Polito had known him since he was 11 years old. Shea looked around, spotted Polito and walked directly to his table. He pulled out a chair and sat down across from him. He looked disgusted.

"Joe," he said, "did you drop that Yuppie fuck in the middle of Russell?"

"Why? Is he still blocking traffic?"

"No. Some kid called it in and I took it. By the time I got there, he was back on his feet. He was okay to drive back to Cambridge, but he didn't look too fucking steady."

"Good. Maybe he'll stay there."

"You don't get it. The kid saw you do it. He gave me a good enough description, I knew it was you. You're just fucking lucky the guy's not pressing charges. If he did, you'd be down at the station right now. You could get a year for that."

"Maybe it's worth it. Fucking dickhead needs to learn some manners if he's going to come around here."

"Maybe, but that's not the point. The point is, my lieutenant hates this shit, the captain hates it, everybody hates it, right up to the fucking mayor.

20

Personally, I'm with you, but that don't mean shit. Davis is supposed to be coming up in the world. A street fight isn't good for public relations. It makes me look bad to my lieutenant, and that's all that fucking matters."

Polito took a deep breath and blew it out in a gesture of helpless frustration. "I know. I wasn't looking for trouble, but that fucking guy's got balls driving through our neighborhood, laying on the horn because he has to wait two seconds for one of us in the crosswalk. Fuck him. You do what you got to do."

"Like I said, no charges. I'm just telling you so maybe you'll think next time before you punch out some Yuppie fuckhead in the middle of the square."

"Okay, I got it. But you're wasting your time. These assholes keep coming around like they own the place, shit's going to happen."

"I got news for you; they do own it. Just like the fucking Brazilians own east Somerville. The people we knew growing up are gone. They're out in Woburn and Wilmington now, driving their fucking mini-vans and drinking lattes. We're the ones who don't belong."

"There's still some of us left."

"Yeah, and you know what? Most of us that are left want these assholes coming around. They got money. Look around. Everybody's fixing up their houses. The schools are getting better. Businesses are moving in. I got two kids in school. I hate these fucking assholes, but I want their money."

"They can keep their goddamn money. This was a great place back when we were kids and nobody had a fucking nickel."

"Yeah, and look what happened. The fucking crackheads nearly took it over. You can't go back."

"No, but you can fight to hold onto what you've got."

"Goddamn it Joe, that's the point. You can't. Not in Somerville. It's not like the old days. Next time, I'll have to arrest you." Shea stood up. His face was dark with anger and something else.

Polito looked up at him mildly. "Do what you got to do."

Shea glared at him for a moment, then turned and walked out. Polito went back to his book and read about 20 pages before Tommy showed up.

Tommy Ahearn was 62, a short, skinny old man with a broken front tooth and a bald head. He wore a scally cap everywhere he went to hide his naked scalp, but the broken tooth showed whenever he smiled, and he smiled a lot. For no reason that anyone could think of, Tommy was a happy man. He had worked at various menial jobs around Davis Square since he dropped out of school at 16. He never had a girl, never married, and he lived alone on his meager earnings.

It was three minutes past 5:00 when he came into the Tavern, just like every other weekday afternoon. Tommy got off his job stocking shelves at the drug store at 5:00 and walked straight down to the Tavern for two beers before he went home to his room in the basement of an apartment building just around the corner. He loved the routine, and Polito knew he could count on it.

The Tavern was getting some business. There were more people at the bar, and Tina had just come in to start serving the tables. Tommy went straight back to Polito's. "Hey Joey," he said, pulling out a chair and sitting down. "What's the news? How's that book? You catch the Bruins last night?"

22

Tommy was the only one who called him Joey. Polito didn't like it, but with Tommy, it wasn't worth the argument. "Hi Tommy," he said. "I met a friend of yours today."

"Oh yeah? Who?" Tommy grinned his broken grin. "I got lots of friends."

"Eileen Merrill."

"Who? Oh, you mean Art's little girl?"

"I wouldn't call her a little girl. She's almost my age, and she's vice president of some company."

"Yeah, yeah. Isn't she something? D'you believe Art with a kid like that."

"She's something alright. I was a little surprised though, when she came in here looking for me. I didn't even know Art had a daughter."

"I know. He doesn't talk about it much, but he's crazy about her, the grandson, too. He goes out there every week. I went with him a couple times." He shook his bald head and frowned. "She came here? - to see you?"

"Yeah, she did. She had some idea I could help her. Somebody must have told her something about me." Polito watched him with an amused grin.

Tommy couldn't meet his gaze. He looked around the room and waved an arm over his head when he saw Tina carrying a tray of drinks. She took them to a table across the room. Tommy stood up and waved. Tina served the drinks to four guys at a table and took their tip. Tommy was still standing with his arm in the air when she turned to him.

"I see you, Tommy. I'll get there when I get there. Sit down." She said it loud enough to carry across the room. Everybody in the place heard it, and some of them laughed, but Tommy didn't care.

He grinned, waved, and sat down. "She'll be here in a minute," he interpreted for Polito, still not looking at him.

"Tell her to bring one for me, okay. This round's on me."

"Really?" Tommy turned to him with reflex eagerness. "That's awful nice of you, Joey. Thanks."

"No problem. You know, I was just thinking I haven't seen Art for awhile."

Tommy nodded violently. "I know. I haven't seen him either, and neither has she."

"When did you see him last?"

"Oh, I don't know. Couple weeks ago."

"Yeah? Where was that?"

"He came over to my place to watch a Bruins game, brought a six-pack. He said it was cheaper than watching at the bar, even if my TV was so old and lousy you can't see the puck most of the time."

"He come over much?"

"Hardly ever. Maybe he just wanted some company."

"Yeah, maybe. Something on his mind?"

"What do you mean?"

"When you watched the game and drank the six-pack. What did you talk about?"

"Oh, nothing – the Bruins and stuff - you know."

Tina brought two beers to the table. She was about 30, a little heavy, with a pretty face, dark unruly hair, and quick humorous eyes.

"Hi Tina," Tommy said, beaming up at her. "How you doing?"

"How'm I doing what?" she said, completing their ritual greeting.

Tommy laughed, delighted as always.

"How'd you know I wanted another?" Polito teased her.

"Your glass was empty – that's how," she said, taking his ten and not even bothering to offer him change. She hustled off to serve another table.

Tommy sipped his beer, closed his eyes, leaned back in his chair and sighed. "Ah, that's good."

"Was Art worried about something?" Polito asked, knowing Tommy would have no problem with the transition.

"No. Why should he be worried?"

"I don't know. Why should he be missing the last week and a half?"

"You going to find him, Joey?"

"I guess I'm going to try. I told her I would. Why'd you get me into this?"

"I didn't know what else to tell her. She was upset."

"Is she close to Art?"

"I guess. He took the bus out there every Wednesday afternoon."

"Out where? Where does she live?"

"Lexington. One of those great big houses, like a mansion. You should see it."

"Yeah," Polito said absently. "She married?"

"Yeah, but I never met the guy. He's always working."

"What about the kid?"

"Great kid – Jake. Art's crazy about him, tells him all these crazy stories from the old days, you know about the mob guys – only he calls them 'the bad guys' – and all the stupid funny stuff they did."

"Stupid, yeah. I don't know how funny they were."

"You got to hear the way Art tells it. It's pretty funny."

"Huh," Polito grunted, thinking of something else. "Art's a Catholic, right?"

"Sure. What else would he be?"

"He go to mass?"

"Oh yeah. St. Clement's, same as me. Only I go Saturday afternoon. Art could have gone to St. Catherine's, but he liked Father Monahan at St. Clement's. I like him, too, but usually Father Desrosiers says it Saturdays."

The Tavern was rapidly filling with the usual after work crowd. They were two deep at the bar and Tina was weaving through the standing room, trying to keep up with the tables. Jerry Lyons and Al Mathews came over to Polito's table and Tommy invited them to sit.

Tommy and Al were big Bruins fans, and they got into a deep discussion on the team's chances. For the first time in ten years they had a half-decent team to talk about, and they made the most of it. Jerry thought they were still a bunch of losers; they wouldn't make the playoffs. Tommy and Al fought him on that, but Polito had little to say. He had another beer while Tommy had his second and left when Tommy went home.

CHAPTER 5

Polito walked home to the house on Morrison, the house he'd lived in almost as long as he could remember. His parents had bought it when he was in second grade. It was built as a two-family, but Joe had unofficially created a small apartment on the third floor when his parents died. That was where he lived. The other two apartments gave him a small income year-round, which he supplemented with his wages from roofing in spring, summer and fall.

He'd taken care of major repairs when he put in the third floor apartment – a new roof, new thermal windows, new furnaces, rebuilt porches, attic insulation, interior paint and minor updates to the existing kitchens and baths. There were none of the Yuppie touches, the granite counter tops, the master bath with Jacuzzi, the top-of-the-line appliances, but it was in good shape and comfortable. Both tenants had been there for years and now paid well below market rent. They liked Joe, liked living there, and they took care of their apartments as if they owned them. His own space on the third floor was three rooms and newer, but not much different than Art Delaney's place. The comparison struck a sour note as he went up the stairs to call Eileen Merrill.

He called on his cell phone from the living room. He could have made the call while walking home, but he hated the people he saw talking on their phones on the street. Whether they were walking or driving, there was something cold and self-absorbed about carrying on a telephone conversation in a public place. His attitude made no sense, even to him, but that didn't change it. He didn't want to be one of them.

"Hello?" a female voice answered.

"Hello. Mrs. Merrill?"

"No, I'll get her." The voice had a trace of a foreign accent.

"Hello?" Eileen Merrill picked up the phone almost immediately.

"Mrs. Merrill? This is Joe Polito. I was wondering if I could see you tonight. I found a couple things at Art's apartment I'd like to talk to you about."

"Yes, Joe. I'm glad you called. Would you like to meet somewhere?"

"I'll just drive out, if that's alright with you. You live in Lexington?"

She paused before answering, but when she did, there was no hesitation in her voice. "That's right, 232 Patriots Drive. Will you be coming out Route 2?"

"Yeah."

"Then get off on Waltham Street and take it right into the center of town."

"Okay."

"Take a left on Mass. Ave. Then just before the Lexington Green, take a right on Merriam. Patriots Drive is your first left. The number is on the mailbox at the end of the drive. You can park around in back by the garage, and there's a back entrance. I'll leave the light on. What time will you be coming?"

"I could be there in half an hour."

"Make it an hour. I have a couple things to do. Okay?"

"I'll see you then."

Polito shaved and brushed his teeth. He changed his sneakers, jeans and sweatshirt for a pair of crepe soled brown leather shoes, tan khakis and a dark blue button down shirt. When he was done, he checked himself in the mirror. The face that frowned back at him was angry and a little confused.

Fortunately his tenant's car was not in the driveway, so Joe didn't have to move it to get to his. Joe had a 15 year old Mustang that he rarely drove in the winter. The car had given him a lot of trouble when he first bought it, used, just after he lost his job with the Somerville PD, but he had a friend who had a shop over the line in Medford who fixed it up and kept it running. It hadn't been out of the driveway in more than a week, so the ten mile run out to Lexington would be good for blowing out the sludge.

Patriots Drive ran low on the slope of a hill overlooking Lexington Green, where the first shots of the Revolution were said to have been fired. The house was as big as Tommy described it. Polito thought at first it was two houses, but saw, when he drove around to the back, that they were joined. The original house, which sat somewhat up the slope from the addition, was a stately brick and slate Victorian. Although the addition was a more modern design, someone had spent a lot of money insuring that its bricks and slates matched those of the old house perfectly in color and size.

When he got out of his car, Eileen Merrill came out the back door and stood under a bright floodlight on the deck. She wore tight designer jeans and a brown yoke-neck sweater. Her hair was pulled back in a loose pony tail, making her look younger than she had when Polito saw her at the Tavern.

"Hi," she said, smiling slightly, as Joe came up the steps. "You find it okay?"

"No problem."

"Come in."

They went through a tiled foyer into a large room that seemed to be a combination office and sitting room. A fieldstone fireplace took up most of one wall. In one corner, a desk with a phone and a laptop was surrounded by shelves and filing cabinets. The books on the shelves were hardbound reference books, probably law. There was a small bar with a refrigerator and sink in another corner, and, in the center of the room, a leather sofa with matching chairs arrayed around a glass coffee table faced the wall of windows that looked out over other houses and down to the Green.

She showed him to one of the chairs and asked if he'd like a drink.

"Sure," he smiled, "bourbon on the rocks."

She went to the bar and looked in one of the cabinets. "Let's see, we have Elijah Craig 12-year-old and Blanton's."

"Both out of my league. Which is better?"

"I don't know. I don't drink bourbon."

"I'll try the Blanton's. I've never heard of it."

"That makes sense," she laughed.

Polito got up and went to the window while she poured. "Nice view," he commented when she brought the drinks.

"Kind of restful, don't you think," she said and sat down at the end of the sofa nearest his chair.

"And historic."

"That too. You know they reenact it every year. I've watched from here a couple times. It always makes me wonder if they had any idea what they were starting."

"I don't think so. If they did, they probably would have gone home and gone to bed."

She laughed and sipped her drink.

"I thought you said you didn't drink bourbon," Joe said, nodding at her glass.

"I don't, but sometimes I like to try new things."

30

"Sometimes I do too."

She let the silence settle over them for a moment while she looked out the window. "You said you found something at my father's place?"

"I did." Joe took the bundle of $100 bills from his pocket and put it on the table. "This was in a shoe in his closet."

She picked up the bundle and examined it. "That's a lot of money for him."

"That's what I thought. Any idea where it might have come from?"

"No idea."

"There was something else." He took the letter from United Catholic Missions from his shirt pocket and unfolded it for her.

She read it and frowned. "It sounds like he was asking about working for them as a missionary."

"Did he ever talk to you about anything like that?"

"Never."

"Was he very religious?"

"Not particularly. He said he went to mass, but he didn't talk about it. I thought it might have been a way to deal with the guilt he felt for things he did when he was younger."

"Maybe. Did he have something like that on his mind?"

"If he did, he didn't talk about it with me." She hesitated. "But ..."

"But what?"

"How well do you know him?"

"He hangs out at the Tavern, a friend of Tommy's, sits at our table sometimes. Seems like a good guy, but I don't really know him any more than that."

"Well, he is a good guy." Her eyes softened with an odd mix of pride and regret. "I hardly knew him growing up. My mother wanted nothing to do with him. She divorced him and we moved out of Somerville when he went to prison. When he got out, my mother made it hard for him to see me, and I was kind of afraid of him. Anyway, it never worked out, and he was just an embarrassing ghost from a dark, shameful past. It wasn't until about 5 years ago that we had any relationship at all. That was when he discovered Jake and Jake discovered him."

She stopped and sipped her drink.

"Tommy told me they're close," Polito said to keep her talking.

"They are." Her expression hardened into a frown. "Jake is closer to his grandfather than he is to me or his father. It's ... We just work too much." Again, she stopped.

"Tommy says Art likes to tell him stories."

"Yes, and Jake loves them."

"Stories about the old Somerville gangs? Kind of rough stuff for a kid, isn't it?"

She managed a rueful smile. "You'd think so, but Art makes them into little fables, where the good guys always win and the bad guys end up looking foolish. He had a new one every week. It seemed like they just bubbled up out of him. I thought he'd never run out."

"Did he?"

"That's what I was going to tell you. If you really knew him, he was a bright, funny old man, and despite everything that happened to him, he was happy. But about a month ago that changed. You asked if he had something on his mind. I think maybe he did. He stopped telling Jake those stories. He was just kind of quiet. I didn't think too much about it, but now I think you might be right; maybe there was something bothering him."

"But he never talked about it?"

"No."

"What about Jake? Do you think he might have said something to him?"

"He might have."

"Why don't you ask him about it?"

"Okay," she said slowly, thinking about it, "but I'll have to be careful; I don't want to worry him."

"No."

Silence settled over them for a moment. Eileen drained the last of the bourbon from her glass and looked at Joe's. "Would you like another? I think I will."

"Why not," he said, handing her the glass.

As she fixed fresh drinks at the bar, she said, "I must have seemed like an alien invasion coming into that bar this afternoon."

Polito smiled to himself. "I don't know," he said. "I think you were kind of exciting. We're all so used to each other, the same old faces. You gave them something to talk about."

She brought the drinks and sat down. "What about you? What did you think?"

"When I looked up, you were heading for my table." He sipped his drink and smiled. "I thought, 'Oh shit, what did I do? What the hell does she want with me?'"

"And when I told you?"

"Then I thought, 'Oh shit, she thinks I'm something I'm not.'"

"But you decided to help me anyway."

"You make it hard to say no."

"Then don't."

Polito stood up and took his drink to the window. "You want what you want when you want it, don't you?" he said with his back to her.

"Doesn't everyone?"

"And your husband?"

"Mark's in New York. It's not his business. He wouldn't be interested."

"And your boy? Jake?"

"Anna has put him to bed in the old house. They know I'm not to be disturbed while I'm down here ... working."

Polito said nothing, staring out at Massachusetts Avenue where it turned at the Green, the direction the redcoats had marched on their way to Concord that fateful day in 1775. After a long silence, he shook his head. "It's not how this is supposed to go."

"I don't have time for that," she said.

He saw her reflection in the window, staring back at him, suspended in space out over a dark, sloping, well-kept lawn. Her lips were slightly parted, her eyes dark and intense. She leaned lightly on her elbow, which rested on the arm of the sofa, giving her body a soft languid posture, as if she was already savoring what was inevitably to follow.

Polito turned and walked toward her. His eyes were serious, almost grim. He sat beside her and pulled her roughly to him. He kissed her with a violence that was nothing like the kiss he'd given Lisa Landry. Her mouth was warm, soft, wet. He pushed her away and looked into her eyes. They were green and deep as an ocean.

"You can't just walk in and take one of us," he whispered, half to himself.

"That's not what I want," she whispered back fiercely. "I want you to take me."

She obediently raised her arms as he pulled the sweater over her head. Her small firm breasts were free beneath it. Polito cupped one in his hand, rolling her nipple between his thumb and index finger. Her eyes closed and she laid her head back on the sofa.

His other hand slid behind her back and pulled her to him with an animal strength that she had never experienced. He softly bit the other nipple, which was puffy and red, waiting for his lips. A breath came from her throat in a deep shuddering moan.

Joe had not had a woman for more than a month. He tore at her jeans with an urgency that would have shredded them had they not slid smoothly from her soft white thighs. She arched her back and raised her hips to allow the delicate triangle of blood red lace to immediately follow. The words he had to say and the person he had to be were carried away on the surging flood of his need.

At some point, his eyes opened and he saw her face. Her eyes were closed and seemed to be rolled up in their sockets. Her mouth was slightly open and slack, allowing her breath to come in short sharp puffs. But in the set of her cheeks and brow, he saw the fear and desperation that drove her passion. At that moment, it could not stop his own, but it slipped into memory, waiting for a better time to haunt him.

CHAPTER 6

The missing persons report on Art Delaney showed up on Sergeant Gianetti's desk without comment - no sticky note from the lieutenant, no follow-up calls. Gianetti looked at it for 30 seconds and classed it a nuisance. It required him to assign an officer to stop by the address and check for anything obvious. Then he could file it and move on to something meaningful. He planned to give it to one of his guys at the next morning meeting, but Officer Chad Reese made that unnecessary when he volunteered.

It was odd that Reese would know about that particular piece of paper. The report had only been filed the day before, joining the hundreds of memos, reports, orders, and other official documents that swirled through the station every day. But the casual chatter among cops and clericals flowed just as thick and fast, and Reese carefully cultivated and maintained his sources. It was also odd for him to volunteer for anything, but the sergeant was not one to look a gift horse in the mouth. He gave Reese the paper and promptly forgot about it.

Reese was a handsome kid from Winter Hill, a rookie with dark brown hair and a neatly trimmed mustache that drooped just slightly at the corners of his mouth. He was just over six feet tall, with a lean build, sharp features, and dark penetrating eyes. In fifteen months on the Somerville force, he had already made a name for himself, and the name was "Asshole," full name "Fucking Asshole." He was cocky and a whiner, without interest in his peers or respect for his superiors, yet ruthlessly political, and a shameless ass-kisser. He was crafty, but not bright. He considered himself a lady's man and kept his blues spotless and pressed. The best thing that could be said about him was that he looked good in the uniform. His lack of popularity among the other cops had given credence and long life to the rumor that he had made the force strictly through the influence of his father the state rep from East Somerville.

Getting out of his cruiser in front of the Elston Street house, he smoothed his shirt and retucked it into his pants. Lisa Landry pulled a sun-bleached curtain aside and looked down from her front window. She thought he looked pretty good and was encouraged when he came to the front door of her building. When she heard him ascend the stairs, she knew what he was there for and began to contemplate all the ways she could help.

Reese knocked hard on Delaney's apartment door. After half a minute, he knocked again, adding loudly, "Art Delaney, you there? Anyone?"

There was silence on the stairs. Reese tried the door. It was locked. He saw no marks of forced entry and nothing of interest on the landing. He started back down the stairs, intending to knock on the doors of the other two tenants, see if they knew anything.

Lisa Landry beat him to it. "He's not there," she said, standing in the open doorway as he arrived at her landing. She had changed into light gray leggings and a long black sweatshirt. Her hip was cocked and she leaned a shoulder against the door frame. One hand held a burning cigarette and a can of beer. She had let her hair down, and her eyes were bright from the beer.

In the dim light, Reese thought she looked alright. "I guess not," he grinned. "You know where he is?"

"Funny," she said, "you're the second person asked me that this afternoon."

"No shit?"

"No shit." She took a tentative step back into the apartment. "You want to come in and talk about it. I don't like talking out here on the stairs."

Reese followed her into the living room, where she had him sit on the sofa. The room was littered with overflowing ashtrays and celebrity magazines. "Sorry about the mess," she said, pushing a few of the magazines into a haphazard pile on the coffee table. "You want a beer, or you on duty?" With a vague grin, she thrust out her chest and saluted.

Reese gave her a toothy smile and looked at his watch. "Lucky me. I'm just off my shift, and I could use a beer."

"I'll be right back," she said brightly and shuffled out to the kitchen.

Reese looked around the room, and a faint sneer curled his lip. In less than a minute he had sized up the woman and her nest. He knew exactly what options lay open to him.

"Yeah, seems like all of a sudden everybody's interested in old Art," Lisa said, coming back into the room and settling herself next to him on the sofa. She put a cold can of beer on the coffee table before him and sat back, crossing her legs. "He's a nice old guy, but what's the big deal?"

"Missing persons report," Reese shrugged. "Routine."

"His daughter looking for him?"

"Yeah, I think it was."

"She sent the other guy, too. Must be worried about the old man. Not like my old man. He was missing most of the time and we were glad. Only thing he ever gave my mother was a lot of bruises and me." She laughed. "I don't know which was worse."

Reese gave her his dimpled grin, the one he had practiced in the mirror and used effectively on many occasions. He could see it work in her eyes. Their alcoholic brightness took on a softer sheen. "Who was this other guy?" he asked.

"Said his name was Joe Polito. Claimed the daughter sent him."

"Did he go in the apartment?"

"Must have. I was just getting home, but I parked outside a few minutes listening to a song on the radio. Nobody went in while I was sitting there, so he must have been up there at least five minutes. I doubt he was standing in front of the door all that time."

"You're a little detective, aren't you?"

She giggled. "I keep my eyes open."

"Then you can tell me what this Joe Polito looked like."

"Of course I can. I got a real good look at him. He was shorter than you, but stocky, kind of rough looking – you know, jeans and sweatshirt - and his hands. His hands were rough and hard, with thick fingers, like he worked with them. He had a wide face and dark hair. He was a little older than you and not as good looking, but not bad."

"I guess you did take a good look at him. How'd you get to talk to him?"

"He was coming down the stairs when I was coming up, and he asked if I knew where Art was."

"But you didn't, right? So what else did he ask?"

"When I saw him last. I told him I heard Art come in a week ago last Saturday – middle of the night."

"That right?"

39

"Yeah, but I didn't tell him everything. I mean, why should I? What's in it for me?"

"What did you want?"

"Me? I'm like Cyndi Lauper. This girl just wants to have fun."

"But you've got to tell me everything. I'm a cop."

"I thought you said you were off duty."

"That's true," he said slowly. "So, you think I should show you some fun, if you're going to tell me what I want to know."

"That's only fair. Anyway, wouldn't you like a little fun?"

"I would, but I'm still in uniform. It wouldn't be right."

"Then take it off."

"How about first you tell me and then we'll see about the fun."

"Okay." She slid closer to him. "What I didn't tell him was that I used to get together with the old guy sometimes for a beer – just for someone to talk to, you know. Sometimes he'd come down here; sometimes I'd go up there. Anyway, about a month ago, I didn't have nothing to do, so I went up and knocked. He came to the door, his eyes all red, like he'd been crying, but he lets me in and starts telling me all this crazy stuff about how the past never dies and some things can't ever be forgiven. And he asks me if I believe in God and stuff, and is it the god of mercy or the eye-for-an-eye kind. I don't even know what I said, but it didn't matter. He was just babbling. After a while he calmed down and I came back downstairs. I didn't think too much about it until he disappeared. And then you guys start coming around. I wouldn't be surprised if you find him floating in the harbor."

Reese listened carefully, watching her, frowning with concentration. "He didn't say what was bothering him?"

"No, it was like some big secret. I kept trying to get it out of him, but he wouldn't say. I thought it might have been about somebody who died. The *Globe* was sitting right there on his table, open to the obituaries. Or maybe it was something he did. You know he was an ex-con, did time in Walpole."

"Yeah, I know. But he wouldn't tell you about it?"

"No. I said he ought to talk to a priest, with all his worrying about god and everything."

"Yeah." Reese was thinking.

"He said they couldn't help."

"But he didn't talk about going to the cops with it?"

"He didn't say. Maybe he should of if it bothered him so much. The funny thing was, he was the nicest old man you'd ever want to meet. It was always 'Hi Lisa, how you doing?' making a joke, holding the door if I had groceries."

"Any friends?"

"Not that came around here. Just one I can think of."

"Who's that?"

"Some weird-looking skinny old guy with a bald head and a broken tooth. I see him walking around Davis all the time. Wears a scally cap."

"How about women?"

She laughed. "I don't think so. Art was getting up there in years, not much interest anymore." She put a hand on his thigh and squeezed gently. "Not like some of us."

"So now you think I owe you a little fun, huh?" He smiled coldly. "Why don't you see what you can do to get me in the mood?"

41

Lisa's hand moved up to his crotch, where she felt him stirring. He leaned back and closed his eyes as she fumbled with his belt and zipper. Getting him in the mood turned out to be quite a bit of work. Reese's only contribution was to grab a handful of hair at the back of her head and use it to guide her, while Lisa had to use every trick she could think of to keep him interested. She soon realized that his image as a lady's man was just that – an image. As soon as he was finally "in the mood," he grunted and shuddered, and then he was done.

Bitter experience had taught her that he would have nothing left for her, but she got up and went into the bathroom to rinse out her mouth anyway, with the faint hope that she would be wrong. That hope vanished when she returned and found him standing in the middle of the room with his pants on and a cell phone to his ear. "Yeah, I'll be right there," he said into the phone and snapped it shut.

"What?" she said. "You've got to go?"

"Afraid so. Emergency over by Union Square. They're calling in a couple extra patrols. I got to pick up my partner and hustle over there. Bad timing. Only good thing about it is the overtime." He was already moving toward the door.

She watched him with a vacant frown. "You want to stop back later, when you get off, so we can … you know, finish?"

"Not tonight. Too late. Maybe later this week. I'll check in and see if old Art has showed up. In the mean time, if he does, give us a call. I got to go."

Before he was down the stairs, Reese was working out how he'd tell this one to the guys at the Harborside, a flashy downtown bar where he liked to hang out. They'd appreciate the cell phone trick, and

Lisa, his disappointed sex toy. It was perfect, just the kind of story he liked to tell.

But Lisa had learned one thing. She knew his name. She pulled the curtain aside and looked out the window as Reese climbed into his cruiser. "Fucking Asshole," she said as the black and white drove off down the street.

CHAPTER 7

There was a bedroom in the new wing of the Merrill house. It was another large room with a view of historic Lexington and included a master bath the size of Polito's living room. The bed was queen-sized, with a mattress of some spongy material Joe had never seen before. After their first round of love-making was over, Eileen and Joe had moved in there to continue.

For several hours, they had hardly spoken. The primitive communication of body to body had been more satisfying than words. But then, when their bodies were spent, words came back to them in the form of questions that could no longer be ignored.

Joe lay on his back, looking up at the ceiling. Eileen lay against him, her head on his chest, with one leg bent over his. With her face turned away, he could not tell if she was awake. They were naked and warm under a down quilt. A table lamp beside the bed threw soft light into the room, but it did not reach into the corners.

"Why me?" he asked softly enough not to wake her if she was asleep.

"You asked me that before," she responded immediately, as if she had been waiting for it.

"Yes, but that was about something else. Or was this part of the plan from the start?"

"I don't plan things like this."

"But they do happen."

She chose to answer a slightly different question. "They do if you want them to."

"Did you want this to happen?"

"After I met you this afternoon, yes. I wanted it to happen." She rolled off him and put her head beside his on the pillow so she could watch his face. "Did you?"

He frowned up at the ceiling. "I don't know. It didn't seem to matter."

"Of course it matters."

"Why? I knew where this was going and I knew I wasn't going to stop it. I didn't want to think about it any more than that."

"Why not?"

"I don't know, god damn it. That's just the way I felt. Why are you the one asking all these questions when I'm the one in the dark?"

"Ask me anything you like."

"Alright." He rolled toward her, so their faces were inches apart, and he looked directly into her dark unblinking eyes. "I asked you this before, too. What about your husband?"

"What about him?" she asked mildly. "Are you worried he's going to come storming in here and shoot you?"

"I'm not worried about a damn thing. I'm just trying to figure out what kind of deal I'm getting myself into."

"Then ask me that, because believe me, Mark has nothing to do with it."

Polito let that sink in for a minute before he muttered, only half joking, "Christ, I'm glad I'm not married to you."

Her expression became very serious, almost sad. "If you were married to me it might be different."

They were quiet for several minutes after that, but neither of them slept. The silence was not uncomfortable, but the questions lingered. Even in the dim light, Joe could see the reckless humor returning to her eyes.

"What about you?" she asked. "Don't you have someone to answer to?"

"No," he said quickly. "Just me."

"Why's that?"

"I don't know," he said carelessly. "Maybe I'm not much good at long term relationships."

"What makes you think that?"

"The fact I haven't had one in 10 years. It's kind of a dead giveaway."

"Have you wanted one?"

"No."

"Well then that's the reason."

"Yeah, I guess."

"Then what do you want?"

"Nothing. I got enough money, a place to live, people to talk to ..."

"Good books to read," she added for him.

"Yeah, that too."

"I saw that book you were reading this afternoon. Kind of unusual for a bar room. Isn't it hard to concentrate – all those Russian names?"

"I like to have people around me. They don't bother me."

"You like Dostoevsky?"

"I like his characters. They've all got crazy ideas, but they live and die by them. Not like us. We might have ideas, but we don't believe them. We live the way everybody else thinks we should."

Joe was surprised to see the humor fade from her eyes again. "You don't live that way, do you Joe?"

"It's hard not to."

"Is that why you read Dostoevsky in a bar room?"

"I don't know. Maybe. You ever read him?"

"I tried *Brothers Karamazov* once, but it was too long. I didn't have time for it."

"I can imagine."

"What do you mean?"

"You don't get to be 'Vice President and Legal Counsel' of some company without putting in the time."

"No," she said slowly, "you don't."

They were quiet again. The room was chilly, but their bodies warmed each other under the thick quilt. The questions began to fade into the dark corners of the room.

Joe had only one more. "Do you want me to go?" he whispered.

"No," she whispered back, pulling his mouth to hers. Her lips were soft and warm, but she kissed him hard, almost desperately. When she released him, her eyes were bright. "But you'd better leave before morning. Jake is awfully sharp. I don't want him asking about you."

"Because you'd have to lie?"

"Because I don't know the answers."

They made love one more time before Joe left.

CHAPTER 8

Polito woke around 9:00, in his own bed. The first thing he was aware of was the faint scent of flowers. It had a strong and pleasant association that took him a moment to place. When he did - when he remembered Eileen, the animal urgency of their first coming together and their explorations under the quilt - he stretched and felt a gentle warmth flow through him. He sat up with a perplexed smile, shook his head and shuffled into the bathroom for a shower.

He put on the same khakis he had worn the night before and a different dress shirt, added a ¾ length coat and knit cap and went down to the street. He walked up College Avenue to a sandwich shop across from the Old Powder House park, where he got coffee and eggs and read the paper.

The girl behind the counter, the boy on the grill and most of the customers were college kids. Polito was 20 years older, but they weren't interested in him and he was only dimly aware of them. With the Tufts campus just a block away, they were part of the environment.

When he finished his leisurely breakfast, he circled the rotary and walked up Warner to St. Clement's at the Somerville Medford line. Like his parents, Polito was a Catholic in name only. But even a nominal Catholic growing up around Davis would have to make a point of it to avoid the church for an occasional Christmas mass or the wedding of a friend. Polito didn't feel that strongly about it. He'd been in the church many times before.

Since the morning mass had concluded a couple hours earlier, he expected to find the church locked, but he walked up the wide steps and tried the door anyway. He was surprised when it swung open. It was quiet inside, deserted, and not much warmer than outside.

A middle-aged man in work clothes was pushing a dry mop up and down the aisles. Joe asked him where he could find Father Monahan. The man looked up through thick glasses with a blank stare, as if he was just waking from a deep sleep.

"Oh, he'd be across the street at the Rectory, probably," he said slowly.

Joe said, "Thanks," and smiled.

The man said, "You're welcome," but his eyes did not seem to meet Joe's.

Joe turned and walked away, but the door had closed behind him before the man went back to slowly pushing his mop along the aisle.

Polito had to ring the bell to be admitted to the Rectory. A stocky woman of about 60, with white hair and a broad flat face ushered him into a small sitting room with upholstered chairs and bookshelves lining the walls. She said she would see if Father Monahan was available.

The room was in a corner of the building, with one window looking out to the church across Warner, the other to a cut-price gas station and car wash across the intersecting street, Boston Avenue. Railroad tracks ran just behind the gas station. Even at mid-morning, traffic was heavy through the intersection.

Father Monahan was a small wiry old man with a full head of white hair and bright blue eyes. He smiled warmly and offered Joe his hand. "I'm Father Monahan. Mrs. O'Connell said you wanted to see me."

Joe shook his hand. "Yes, Father. My name is Joe Polito and I'd like to ask you some questions about one of your parishioners. I'm not certain you even know him, but I understand he was a regular at your Sunday mass – Art Delaney?"

A small frown passed quickly over Father Monahan's face. "Yes, I know Art. Maybe we should talk in my study."

Joe followed him up the central staircase and down a hall to another small room with a desk, several chairs and more shelves of books. The priest sat in a swivel chair behind the desk and Joe took one of the chairs facing him. Father Monahan's smile was polite but curious.

"Why are you interested in Art Delaney?" he asked.

"Apparently Art is missing. His daughter asked me to look for him."

"I see." The frown returned. "But you're not a policeman. Have the police been notified?"

"His daughter filed a missing persons report, but she feels they won't have time to do very much about it. She's hoping I can do more."

"Is she paying you for your time?"

"No. I'm doing it because Art is a friend of mine."

Father Monahan nodded. "When you say 'missing,' what do you mean? How long has he been gone?"

"As far as I can tell, he hasn't been in his apartment for about a week and a half. The woman who lives downstairs from him said she heard him come in that Saturday night and hasn't heard or seen him since. His daughter hasn't heard from him since the Thursday before that, two weeks ago today."

"Now that you mention it, he wasn't at mass this past Sunday. And you're right; he was very faithful in his attendance."

"Was he there the week before?"

"Yes he was."

"Then that was the last time anyone I've talked to saw him. Did you get a chance to talk with him then?"

Father Monahan looked down at the green blotter on his desk and scowled. "I spoke with him briefly," he said, before he looked up.

"What did he say? Was he upset? Did he talk about going anywhere or doing anything?"

"This is difficult, Mr. Polito." The priest folded his hands on the blotter. "You see, I recently took Mr. Delaney's confession, a very personal and private communication. I would like to help, but I am concerned about breaking that trust. So much of what we talked about outside of the confessional relates directly to the issues of conscience that he confessed to me there."

"That doesn't surprise me, Father. His daughter said he seemed troubled in the last month or so. She thinks it's related to his disappearance."

"I don't doubt that, but it doesn't change my obligation to him."

"I wouldn't ask you to, but if you could help us with anything he said apart from his confession ..."

They stared at each other for a long moment. Joe had an irrational fear that the keen blue eyes of the priest were burrowing into his head, discovering his secret sins – specifically, his most recent sins of the flesh with Art Delaney's daughter. But Father Monahan was not interested in Joe Polito's conscience. He was examining his own, trying to determine where his duty lay in this unusual situation.

"Perhaps if I spoke to his daughter," he finally said, spreading his hands apologetically. "It's not that I don't trust you. I suppose I'm just buying time, really, but I don't quite know what to do."

"I understand. I guess I could see if she could come in this evening," he said reluctantly, then brightened when he remembered her card. "No, wait. I have her phone number at work. You could call her there."

"Alright. I guess that might help."

Joe pushed the card across Father Monahan's blotter with the business side up. There was nothing incriminating about her home phone number on the back, but he was still feeling uncharacteristically superstitious. Father Monahan picked up a cordless phone from its cradle on his desk and punched in the number. His expression was blank while the phone rang, but came to life when someone picked up on the other end.

"Yes. This is Father Monahan at St. Clement's Church in Medford. I wonder if I could speak to Eileen Merrill.... It's a personal matter.... Thank you."

He waited again.

"Hello, Ms. Merrill. This is Father Monahan. I'm here at St. Clement's with Mr. Polito who, I understand, is helping you look for your father, Art Delaney.... Yes, your father is one of my parishioners, and I'm worried about him too. That's why I'm calling. Mr. Polito is asking questions that I can't answer without coming dangerously close to violating the sacred privacy of the confessional.... I understand, but I can't disclose anything your father told me there. What I can do, with your permission, is to tell him whatever I know that wasn't part of his confession.... Good. That's what I thought you'd say, and I agree. Would you like to be included? I can put you on speakerphone."

Father Monahan pushed a button on the phone and placed it in the middle of his desk. "Can you hear me, Ms. Merrill?"

"Yes, very clearly. Hello, Joe."

It was her voice, but metallic and impersonal coming through the phone's tiny speaker. "Hello, Eileen," Joe replied carefully, hoping to hide the flash of frustration he felt at this awkward conversation – over the phone in the presence of a priest – with someone he'd last talked to while they held each other in a warm bed.

Fortunately, Father Monahan took over. "Your father attended mass a week ago last Sunday, Ms. Merrill. Mr. Polito tells me that was the last time anyone saw or heard from him. One of the reasons I'm telling you this is because he seemed quite agitated. I remember it worried me at the time."

"What did he say?" Eileen asked, her voice sharp with concern.

"Unfortunately, I was in the receiving line as the worshipers left the service. There was only time for a few words. He took my hand and said something like 'Thank you, Father, for all you've tried to do for me. I can never deserve it, but please pray for me.' I promised him I would and then he had to move along so that I could greet the others in line. A couple minutes later, I saw him get into a big black car that pulled up, apparently just to pick him up."

"Did you see who was in the car?" Polito asked.

"No. It stopped in the middle of the street because there was no place to pull into the curb. Somebody honked and I looked up. I just caught a glimpse of Art getting in the car."

"Could you tell anything about the make or year of the car?"

"Fairly new, and big. That's all I remember."

Polito leaned over the desk toward the phone. "Eileen, any idea who that would be?"

"No. Tommy is the only one of my father's friends I've met, and I'm pretty sure it couldn't have been him. I was hoping it might give you an idea."

"Not really, but it's one more thing to look for. Father, you said Art was agitated. How? What he said doesn't sound all that upset."

"I guess it was the way he said it. He was so serious, almost grim, and I guess I was thinking of all the problems that he'd been struggling with. It seemed like he was giving up."

"What problems?" Eileen asked harshly.

Father Monahan focused his steady serious gaze on Polito. "This is where I have to be careful. A few weeks ago, your father made his confession. I believe it was the first time he had done so in many years. Since then, I've met with him twice to counsel him on issues of conscience and faith. He had asked my help to deal with a burden of guilt and shame that he found almost unsupportable. Our traditional answers – confession, prayer, faith – did not seem to help. In fact, I had the sense that the burden had continued to grow. That was probably why I found his few words that day ... alarming."

Polito returned Father Monahan's steady stare. "And the reason for his guilt was something he confessed to you?"

"That's right."

"And you can't tell us anything about that."

"No."

Polito frowned. After a moment of silence, he said, "Did you know that Art had sent a letter to a Catholic missionary outfit asking about working for them?"

"No, not specifically. It was one of many ideas that came up in our conversations. I think he felt the need to do something extraordinary to atone for the sin that weighed on his conscience. I didn't know he'd actually contacted them."

"Did he ever mention suicide?" Eileen's voice was low and hoarse.

"Yes, I'm afraid he did. I told him that would only add to the burden on his soul, but I don't think he put it out of his mind entirely."

A low groan came through the phone.

Joe moved on. "Did he mention some money he'd come into?"

"No. I got the impression that he had very little."

Joe nodded. "Is there anything else you can tell us that might help us find him?"

"Not that I can think of. Most of our conversations were about faith and forgiveness, spiritual issues, not the kind of thing that would help very much."

"Eileen, do you have any other questions?"

"No. But thank you Father. I really appreciate the help you gave my father, even if it ... wasn't enough."

They said their goodbyes and Joe promised to call her later. When they'd hung up, Joe stood up to go, but he had one more question. "How did you know that was really Art's daughter, Father? I could have had someone prepped for the call."

"Sure you could have, but I would have known. One of the things I didn't want to mention with her on the phone was that she and her son Jake were a big part of Art's problem. In both of our counseling sessions, they were what he talked about most. I think he could have faced his guilt if it had only fallen on him, but he believed his sin was so unforgivable that it would stain them too, and that he couldn't face. The sins of the father, I guess."

CHAPTER 9

Joe got home just after noon. He sat in the front room and tried to read. He didn't want to go to the Tavern, but he couldn't concentrate at home. It was too quiet. When he finished reading a page, he looked back and realized he didn't know what he'd read. By mid-afternoon, he was too antsy to sit there anymore. He went down to the street, walked to the drug store and found Tommy in his red smock, immersed in rearranging the women's hair products.

"Hey Tommy," he said, interrupting Tommy's concentration.

Tommy blinked. "Oh, hi Joey. How's it going?"

"Good, good. Sorry to bother you while you're working, but I got a couple questions I thought you might be able to answer."

"Sure." Tommy grinned his broken grin. "I'm good at answers. What about?"

"Art Delaney. He used to run around with the mob, right?"

"Yeah, I guess. Only they weren't a mob then, just a bunch of guys."

"He see any of those guys lately?"

"I don't think so. Most of them are dead."

"Hasn't been getting into anything illegal?"

"No way. Art cleaned up his act from the day he got out of prison. He wouldn't screw up now."

"I didn't think so either. What about back before he went in. Who was he running with?"

"Jeez, that's a long time ago. I guess he hung out mostly with Pat Sheehan, back before Pat got big."

"Pat Sheehan," Joe repeated thoughtfully. "He's still alive, isn't he?"

Tommy looked pained. "Yeah, but I hear he's pretty sick. Not supposed to last too long."

"Still lives here in town, though, right?"

"Yeah, over by Union Square, I think. Haven't seen him for a couple years. Used to have a big place just off Walnut - Munroe Street, big pink house with one of those fancy black iron fences, bushes, gardens - everything. Probably still there. I hear he's got the cancer, you know. His next move's to the cemetery."

"That's too bad. I guess Pat's not running things anymore then?"

"He got out years ago. He was lucky. Most of those guys got killed one way or the other."

"Yeah, but him and Art made it through the wars."

"Not Art. He was never in it. He was in Walpole the whole time."

"When did he go in?"

"Must have been '80 – no, '81. I remember, it was right after Christmas. There was going to be a big trial, but Art took it all, confessed before the trial even started. Everybody said it was his Christmas present to Pat and the other guys who could have done time too."

"Manslaughter, right?"

"That's what they called it, but it was just a barroom fight. Somebody got stabbed. Nobody knew who had the knife, but Art said it was him, even said he started it. The DA was pissed. He wanted to get more of them, but after that there wasn't much to get them with. He got Art good, though – ten years."

"So he got to sit out the whole gang war?"

"Oh yeah. It was over by the time he got out. Pat was on top by then and most of the action was happening in Boston anyway. Pat would have given him something, but Art didn't want any part of it. He changed in prison. He was a better person when he came out, and that doesn't happen very often."

"He ever say what changed him?"

"Just that he had a lot of time to think. He didn't like to talk about it."

At the end of the aisle, a fat man with curly black hair stopped and peered at them frowning. The man wore the same red smock Tommy wore, just a bigger size. Joe saw him and said, "Thanks, Tommy. I better let you get back to work."

"No problem. See you at the bar after I get off."

"Not tonight. I got things to do."

When Joe left the drug store, he walked across the street to a little park next to a blacktop basketball court. He sat on one of the benches and made a call from his cell phone. Going through the information operator cost him a dollar, but he didn't feel like hunting down a phone book. Patrick Sheehan was listed. The operator gave him the number and put him through.

"Hello?" A woman's slightly tremulous voice answered.

"Hello. Is Pat there? This is Joe Polito."

"Oh, yes, alright. I'll see if he's awake."

"Yeah?" a hoarse, rumbly voice came through the phone. "What d'you want?"

"Pat, I met you ten years ago. Joe Polito."

"I remember. I wouldn't have answered the phone if I didn't. You were a Somerville cop. They bounced you for beating the shit out of some crackhead, right?"

"That's me."

"You got fucked. What do you want?"

"I'm looking for Art Delaney."

There was a long pause before Sheehan said, "So?"

"So I heard you were friends back in the old days. I thought you might know something about where he is or why he disappeared."

"I know lots of shit. That don't mean I'm going to tell you about it. You want to talk, come over to my place. I see your face, maybe we'll talk."

"When?"

"Any time. I'm not going anywhere."

Joe rode the Highland Avenue bus to Walnut Street and walked down the hill to Munroe. Through the naked branches of trees that lined the street, he could see over East Cambridge and across the river to the Boston skyline. Pat Sheehan's house was a big pink Victorian on the corner. Just as Tommy had remembered, it was surrounded by well-tended gardens and lawns sloping down to a low retaining wall of heavy granite blocks laid neatly along the edge of the sidewalk. An ornate wrought iron fence grew out of the granite. The fence was painted the same shiny black as the Lincoln Town Car parked on the long driveway that flanked the house. Joe climbed the steps to the porch and rang the bell.

The woman who came to the door was about sixty. She had white hair bobbed at the jaw line and wore a gray cardigan sweater over a pink blouse. She was medium height and wide but not fat, and her face was wrinkled with a pleasant smile.

"Yes?" she said.

Joe didn't know if she was Sheehan's wife or his housekeeper. "I'm Joe Polito," he said, taking no chances. "I'm here to see Pat Sheehan."

"Hello, Mr. Polito." She extended her hand. "Pat said you'd be stopping by. It's nice to meet you. I'm Rose Sheehan. Come in."

Pat Sheehan had schemed, fought and murdered his way to the top of the Somerville mob through the gang wars of the eighties. Joe knew he had been a very dangerous man and figured he probably still was. As Rose Sheehan led him through a foyer lined with painted porcelain knick-knacks, pictures in gilt frames, and spindly carved wooden tables, he tried to put it all together – this pleasantly faded lady with her fussy old house and the vicious mob boss. They didn't seem to fit.

She opened a door and ushered Polito into a warm and stuffy sitting room at the back of the house. Pat Sheehan was sitting on a sofa, watching television. A fuzzy pink blanket covered him from shoulders to feet.

"Pat," Rose said, "Joe's here."

"I know. I'm not deaf yet, for Christ's sake." It sounded like the kind of ritual friction that passes almost unnoticed between two people who have been together a long time. Sheehan pushed the blanket aside and clicked off the TV with a remote. He stood up and Joe could hardly recognize the man he'd met years before. Then, Pat Sheehan had been tall and thickly built, with a broad Irish face, dark, deep-set eyes and a full head of hair. Now he was stooped and stick thin. His face was pinched, his eyes yellow and rheumy, and his hair was thin wisps of white that floated over his pink skull like dandelion fluff. He gave Joe a thin smile. "Hello, Joe. Come in and sit down. Sorry it's so god damn hot in here. Seems like I got no blood anymore. Throw your coat on a chair."

Polito shrugged out of his heavy coat and Rose said softly, "I'll take it."

As Joe was taking a seat near Sheehan and Rose was leaving with the coat, Pat said, "And bring us a couple beers, Rosie."

Rose turned and frowned at him. "Now, Pat ..."

"Jesus Christ, one beer isn't going to kill me."

"Alright," she said. "But just one."

"Yeah, yeah."

Rose left and the two men sat. "May not kill me," Pat said, "but it'll taste like piss. With this chemo, nothing tastes right anymore."

"Sorry to hear you're sick."

"Yeah, but the cancer's not so bad, it's the fucking cure that's killing me." He shook his head. "What the hell. I buried most of my enemies. I can't bitch. What'd you want?"

"Art Delaney. He's missing and his daughter asked me to look for him. There's a couple things I thought you might be able to help with."

"Why should I?" The old man looked at him with sour distrust.

"I heard you two ran together before he went to Walpole, that he lay down for the DA on that one and did you a big favor. I thought maybe you owed him something."

The look of distrust turned to anger. "That's between me and him, none of your fucking business."

"It wouldn't be if he was here," Joe said pointedly, "but he's not."

Sheehan was silent for a minute. He finally said, "The daughter wants him found, huh? Well, that's a good thing. I thought maybe she'd be glad to have him out of the way, just a fucking embarrassment."

"She wants him found."

"Even if it kills him?"

"Who the hell is going to kill a harmless old man like Art?"

"You fucking punks. You think we were always old and harmless? We owned this fucking town. Guy like you couldn't've ordered a beer at Tommy Haggarty's place. You'd have been bleeding in the gutter in two minutes."

"That was the old days. Tommy Haggarty's place got shut down when I was still in high school."

"Maybe some of us haven't got the message. Maybe some of us still got some balls. And maybe some of you punks sticking your nose in our business could still wind up bleeding in the gutter."

Rose came in with two glasses of beer and a bowl of potato chips. She carried them on a tray, which she put down on a coffee table in front of Pat. She picked up one of the glasses and handed it to Polito.

She said, "Don't listen to him, Mr. Polito. He's really very glad to have your company. It's just the chemo that makes him grumpy."

"I'm not grumpy, god damn it. And don't treat me like a little kid."

"I'm just saying you won't be having any more visitors if you keep growling at them."

"Yeah, yeah."

When she left the room, Rose closed the door quietly behind her. Sheehan held the glass of beer and looked into it with a sour expression. "She drives me up the fucking wall, but if I didn't have her I wouldn't put up with this shit for ten minutes. I'd eat a bullet and be done with it. You married?"

"No."

"Well, you're still young. Only thing I can tell you is it's a mixed bag. You give up your freedom. You can't just do what you want anymore, but you get a reason to do what you do." He glared at Polito as if he expected him to laugh at an old man's foolishness and sentimentality. When he saw that Polito was watching and listening intently, he went on. "I mean it. Dying like this – a little at a time – it's no fucking picnic. You lose the hair; you can't eat; you get weak. I can hardly get up the fucking stairs anymore. One of these days I'm going to wake up and not be able to get out of bed. And then I'll still have to wait weeks or months – who knows – until this fucking thing chokes the last breath out of me. I'd be dead already if it was up to me. But I'll lie there and take it because that's what Rose wants. She's not going to let me off easy and she's not going to let me feel sorry for myself, because that's what she believes. It doesn't make one god damn bit of sense, but there's not a fucking thing I'd do to change it."

Joe waited until he was sure that Sheehan had finished. "When'd you get married?" he asked.

"Twenty years ago. Just before I retired." His thin lips twisted up in a wry smile. "No connection though."

Joe laughed.

Sheehan's smile faded. "Art was having a hard time. Maybe it got to a point he had enough."

"Maybe." Polito seized the opening. "There was something on his mind, something he felt guilty about. That's what I wanted to ask you. It could be something from the old days you were talking about. Anything from back then that might have given him a guilty conscience?"

"What are you asking – if I know about some shit Art was into thirty years ago he might not be too proud of? You writing another fucking gangster book?"

"No book. I wouldn't give a shit about what you guys were into except I think it might help me find him. So let's get to the point. Do you know where he is?"

"No." He said it flatly and with finality. "I don't even know if he's still alive. And anyway, if he went off somewhere to get his head right, who are you to say he can't? He's got a fucking right."

"Might even be a good thing, huh? If the thing he was worried about was something that involved you."

That made Sheehan mad. His face turned a deep red, almost maroon. "You think I'm worried about me?" he sputtered in his hoarse voice. "What's done is done. Art could go to the cops with every god damn thing I ever did and it wouldn't make two shits difference to me. The cops can't do anything to me now. God's going to take care of that."

"Maybe for you. Art didn't think God could handle it for him."

"He listened to the fucking priests too much."

"They couldn't help him find any peace."

"That's his problem. I don't know where the hell he is, and I'm not going through all the shit we did thirty years ago because you think he might be worried about it now."

Sheehan took a sip of his beer and looked at it with disgust. "God damn stuff tastes like donkey piss."

He put the glass back on the coffee table and slumped against the cushions of the sofa. His head fell back, his eyes stared up at the ceiling and his mouth hung open for a moment. He looked dead, but his lungs issued a breathy sigh. When he brought his tired gaze back to Joe, his voice was hoarse and low. "You don't know what you're getting into. You're not doing Art any good looking for him. I'm telling you to fucking back off – for him, for you, even for his daughter and her son. Somebody's going to get hurt with all this digging around in the past. It's dead and buried. Let it rest."

"So there is something," Polito said.

"God damn it, you're not listening," Sheehan said, but there was no force to it. "You don't even know if he's still alive."

"No," Joe said, "but I'll find out. And the only way to do it is to keep tracking him. So, where'd you drop him off a week ago last Sunday?"

Sheehan frowned up at the ceiling. "What the fuck are you talking about?"

"You picked him up in front of the church, right? Where'd you drop him?"

"You're too god damn nosy, Polito. No wonder you got booted."

"Maybe I am, but there's nothing I can do about it. That's the last time anybody saw him. What's the answer?"

"You fucking pain in the ass. I took him back to his place so he wouldn't have to walk. Big fucking deal."

"Since when are you a taxi service?" Joe said, and immediately regretted it.

"Get the fuck out of here, Polito. I'm not going to sit here and play 20 questions with some busted cop."

"I'm going, but there's one more thing. You know where Art would have got his hands on some serious money?"

Sheehan looked at him. The whites of his eyes weren't white. They were a ghastly mix of yellow and red. "No," he said, "I don't."

"I thought he might have told you about it or even got it from you. I found it when I was looking through his apartment."

"He left it behind, huh?"

"Yeah."

"That's not good."

"No."

65

CHAPTER 10

When Rose Sheehan showed Polito out, she stepped out onto the porch with him. Polito had his coat on, but he shivered coming out of the overheated parlor into the sharp wind. Rose, in her thin sweater, didn't seem to notice. She put a hand out and gently squeezed his wrist.

"Thank you for coming, Mr. Polito. Pat doesn't get many visitors anymore, and he needs the distraction."

"Well, I was glad to get the chance to talk to him," Joe said. "He's still pretty sharp."

"Oh yes, his mind's alright. But sometimes I don't think his judgment is very good." She paused and looked up at him with open speculation and a trace of embarrassment. "I heard some of what you were talking about. I think you're right to keep looking for Mr. Delaney. That poor man needs help if anyone ever did. Pat would be looking for him himself if he was well. I just don't think he trusts anyone but himself for that kind of thing."

"How do you know Art Delaney?"

"I've known him for years, as long as I've been with Pat. Art was one of the only ones from the bad old days that Pat kept in touch with. We didn't see him often, but I liked him. He was always such a gentle, happy man. That's why I was so upset the last time he visited. He just seemed like his heart was breaking."

"When was that?"

"About two weeks ago. He came over and talked to Pat. They both got so upset, I couldn't help overhearing some of what they were saying."

"What? What did they say?"

"I don't know if it will help, but at one point they were shouting, almost like they were crying. Pat said: 'Let it go. She's dead now. You can't do her any good.' Then Art said: 'It's not for her,' and Pat said: 'Then who. There's no one left.' Art said: 'We are.' Then I couldn't hear anymore."

"Who were they talking about?"

"I don't know. I thought maybe you would."

"I don't, but I'm going to find out."

"I hope you do, and don't worry about Pat. I know what he was. Maybe he's paying for what he did, or maybe it's just bad luck. I don't know, but one way or the other, I know he has to face it, and I have to face it with him."

Joe looked into her bright blue eyes. "I'm not trying to make either of you face anything, but I can't promise you it won't happen."

"Well, don't you worry about that."

Joe walked up the street to Highland, but continued on past the bus stop. He walked the two miles back to Davis.

CHAPTER 11

Tommy showed up at the Tavern a few minutes past 5:00, just as he always did, but he was uncomfortable knowing Joe wouldn't be there. He didn't know where to sit. It was true that he had lots of friends at the Tavern, but he always sat at Joe's table. As he walked up to the Tavern's big black and red door, he considered whether he should sit at Joe's table alone until someone he knew came along and sat down, or sit at some other table. It had not occurred to him that someone else might have taken Joe's table, and he was shocked when he walked in and saw a young man with a mustache sitting alone at the table in back.

The young man was not a regular, not someone Tommy recognized, but the man seemed to recognize him. He smiled and waved, inviting Tommy over to the table. Tommy walked uncertainly past the bar, even forgetting to say hello to Tim.

The man leaned back in his chair, smiling up at Tommy. "You're Tommy Ahearn, right?"

Tommy nodded. His face was puzzled, his mouth hanging slightly open, his eyes blank.

"Sit down. Have a beer. I've been waiting to talk to you."

Tommy pulled out a chair and sat, never taking his eyes from the man's face, which maintained its relaxed smile as if it was permanent.

"My name's Chad Reese," the man said extending his hand across the table.

Tommy put limp fingers into the man's hand and muttered, "Hi."

Reese looked around for Tina, caught her eye and signaled for two beers. "I'm a cop," he said. "I mostly work East Somerville, but I got the missing persons report on Art Delaney. I heard you're a friend of his."

"Yeah," Tommy answered tentatively.

"Well, I heard you stop in here after work, so I thought I would too. See if you could help me find him."

Tommy watched him with the same blank expression.

Reese's smile slipped a bit. "You know anything about where he's at, what he's been up to?"

"I don't think so. I ..."

"Yeah?" Reese said eagerly. "What?"

"Nothing." Tommy shook his head negatively. "I haven't seen him in a couple weeks."

"When was the last time?"

"Friday night, two weeks ago."

"Where?"

"My place. We watched a Bruins game."

"What'd he talk about?"

"Nothing much – the Bruins."

Tina put the drinks on the table. Reese gave her a ten and told her to keep it. Tommy picked up his beer, smiled shyly and said, "Thanks."

"Sure," Reese nodded, but he wasn't smiling anymore. "But you got to help me out here. There's some talk Art might have known something about a crime, that he was worried about it. If he told you about it, you've got to tell me, or else you'd be guilty, too."

"He didn't say nothing about any crime."

"But did he seem worried?"

"I don't know. Not really. Maybe a little quiet, you know."

"But he never said why that was?"

"No."

Reese stared hard at him. "You'd better not be lying, Tommy. That could get you in a lot of trouble."

"I'm not lying."

Reese sipped his beer without taking his eyes off Tommy. "Maybe he was down because someone died," he suggested.

"Maybe," Tommy agreed.

"He go to any funerals lately?"

"I don't know. He didn't say anything about it."

"I thought you were his best friend. Doesn't seem like he told you much about what was going on with him."

"We didn't talk about stuff like that. We just got together to watch a game and have a few beers, a few laughs. Art was a funny guy."

"But not lately."

"No."

"What about this guy, Joe Polito. He looking for him too?"

"Maybe. I guess so."

"You guess so," Reese snorted contemptuously. "You know so. Don't you?"

Tommy nodded, his brow furrowed with worry.

"What the fuck does Polito want out of it?"

"Nothing," Tommy protested. "He's just doing it for Art's little girl."

"His daughter, Eileen Merrill?"

"Yeah."

"Why? She paying him?"

"I don't know."

Reese looked disgusted. "What do you think?"

"About if she's paying him?"

"About any of it."

"I don't know," Tommy shrugged helplessly. "It seems kind of strange."

"Strange," Reese repeated with an angry sneer. "You're god damn right it's strange. You see Polito, you tell him to keep his fucking nose out of this. It's official police business, and I don't give a shit what kind of deal he's got with Delaney's daughter. He's out of it."

Reese got up and walked out.

Al Mathews came over to the table. "Hey Tommy. Who was that asshole? He give you a hard time?"

"He said he's a cop," Tommy said, staring at the door where Reese had just disappeared, "but he didn't act like one. He bought me a beer."

Tommy took a drink from his glass and looked at it frowning. "It doesn't taste right when you don't like the guy who bought it."

CHAPTER 12

When Joe Polito got back to his apartment, he made a couple calls. One was to Eileen Merrill. It was answered by the same vaguely foreign female voice he'd heard the last time he called. She told him that Mrs. Merrill had some evening appointments and wouldn't be home until late. Joe left his name and number, but no particular message.

The other call was to Paul Shea. This one was answered by a young boy's voice. Joe asked for Paul and heard the receiver bang on a hard surface.

"Dad," the kid yelled, "phone's for you."

"Hello?"

"Hi Paul, it's Joe."

"Hi Joe." Shea sounded slightly surprised. "What's up?"

"I need to talk to you tonight. You got a few minutes?"

"Yeah, but not right now. We're just sitting down to dinner. How about I meet you in an hour for a beer."

"Fine, but not the Tavern this time. Too many people know us. Maybe that place in Porter across from the Shopping Center, you know the one – mostly college kids. I can't think of the name of it. Shouldn't be too packed on a weeknight."

"I know the one. Meet you in an hour."

The bar was grafted onto a restaurant that claimed to be famous for its burgers. It was dimly lit and busy with a mixed crowd of students and young professionals. Paul and Joe sat in a booth as far removed from the crowd as they could get in the big room, but it wasn't necessary for privacy. There were people all around them, but they were all busy with their own business, moving, talking, trying to impress each other, getting drunk, trying to wash away another day of work or study or nothing. None of them paid any attention to the cop and the ex-cop. The smell of beer was strong and familiar.

"I was going to call you, anyway," Paul said before Joe told him what he wanted.

"What about?" Joe frowned.

"I thought you deserved a warning."

"Like yesterday?"

"Quit busting my balls. You know I was just doing my job. This is different - someone asking questions about you, you and Tommy."

"What kind of questions?"

"Who you were; where you hang out; history – that kind of stuff."

"Who's asking?"

"Another cop, Chad Reese. His name mean anything to you?"

"I think I might have heard of him. Son of Ed Reese, right?"

"That's him. He came on about a year ago - snotty punk thinks he owns the whole department. If it was someone else, I wouldn't think twice about it. With him, it's trouble."

"Why the interest in me and Tommy?"

"Something about a missing persons report. He said you were messing around in it, fucking up his investigation. He had your name and Tommy's description. So, you tell me, what's this big personal interest in a missing persons report that should've been mine to check out, anyway?"

"No idea," Joe shrugged, but his eyes were blank, focused in on his thoughts. "What'd you tell him?"

"I told him how you got kicked off the force. He knew the story, but hadn't put it together with the name. I said you were a thick-headed jerk with a bad temper, and I told him about Tommy. I told him you both hang out at the Tavern."

"Doesn't sound like much. Why is that trouble?"

"Because he's too interested. That report should be worth one stop at Art's place, but this guy – who doesn't fucking work himself to death on police business – all of a sudden, he's running down half-assed leads and making loud noise about some ex-cop getting in his way. He must have some kind of stake in it."

"Yeah, but what?" Joe muttered, half to himself.

"I thought you might know."

Joe shook his head and frowned. "No clue."

"Well, the point is: watch out for this guy. He's a fucking asshole and a loose cannon. I've got no idea what he might do."

"Got it, Paul. Thanks. Now it's my turn. I need all the old stories about Pat Sheehan from the time before he took over, anything he might have been in on that wasn't strong enough to take to court - informant chatter, bullshit, legend. I don't give a shit how flimsy it is. It's not going anywhere."

Shea grimaced. "Shit. You're talking 30 years ago. We were 10. I can look in the files, but you'd be better off talking to one of the old guys that was working back then."

"That's not a bad idea. Got any suggestions?"

"Yeah. Go talk to Walt Gorman. He retired about five years ago, but he's still around. I think he put in almost 40 years, so he would have been on the force back then."

"Walt. I remember him, big guy, kind of fat face, no hair on top."

"That's him. Used to live over near Magoun. Probably still does."

CHAPTER 13

Magoun Square is a collection of bars, restaurants and small businesses clustered around the intersection of Broadway and Medford Street. The ethnic identity of the restaurants gives a clear picture of the neighborhood. There's Chinese, Italian, Brazilian, Irish, etc. – a very eclectic mix. The Italians and Irish are old-time Somerville. The Brazilians and everybody else are more recent. It's all working class and they seem to get along. Joe liked it better than his own neighborhood, where he was beginning to feel like an outsider.

It's only a mile from Davis, sitting right on the Somerville/Medford line at the base of Winter Hill, but its location makes it transitional. The Yuppies and the Tufts students aren't as significant as they are around Davis. There are some, but they form a respectful minority, allowing the working class majority to continue to define the character of the streets. At the same time, the area seems to escape the blight of the teenage gangs that hang out around Mystic Avenue less than half a mile away.

Walt Gorman lived in the two-family house his parents bought when he was six. It sat on a quiet side street off Medford, just a couple blocks from the square. Joe walked from Porter. It wasn't far, but it was chilly. The slush that lined the sidewalks was turning hard and he had to watch for patches of ice where it had melted and refrozen on the concrete, waiting to slip his legs out from under him and dump him on his ass.

It was just a few minutes past nine when he walked up the cracked cement steps onto the porch and rang the bell marked Gorman. The house was clad in faded green vinyl and the porch sagged a bit, but new double-pane windows had been installed sometime in the past ten years, and the paint on the porch floor was new enough not to show much wear. Joe thought the house looked comfortable.

A light showed through the lace behind the glass panel of the front door, and the street was quiet enough for Joe to hear footsteps coming down the short hall. Joe recognized Gorman when he opened the door. As he had said, Gorman was tall and heavy and balding. His face had sagged some, and the bulk that used to be solid had turned a little mushy, but generally, not that different than what Joe remembered.

Gorman didn't recognize him. "Yes?" he said without any particular warmth.

"Hello, Walt. I'm Joe Polito. We used to work together."

Gorman peered at him. "Yeah. Okay. I remember you now. What can I do for you?"

"I'm looking for a friend of mine, a guy you might have run across, Art Delaney."

"I know who he is. Haven't seen him in years. What do you mean, 'you're looking for him'?"

"He kind of went missing a couple weeks ago. Hasn't been to his apartment, hasn't talked to his daughter or any of his friends. The reason I wanted to talk to you, there was something bothering him from the past, probably from way back before he went to Walpole. Most likely, it was some kind of crime from when he was running around with Pat Sheehan and that bunch, something that never got closed, probably something pretty ugly. I thought you might have some ideas."

"Huh," Gorman grunted noncommittally, as if he was just taking it in. "A lot of ugly shit went down back then that never got closed. I guess I could go through some of it if you got the patience to listen to a bunch of tired old bullshit. I got nothing better to do."

"Great," Joe said. "You want to go up to the square. I'll buy you a beer."

"Not tonight. I got babysitting duties. The grandson's sleeping in the back room. I think there's a couple beers in the fridge, though."

Gorman led him through the front room, where he shut off the TV in the middle of a comedy show. The canned laughter died in mid-chuckle. The house was full of fussy old furniture, but everything was neat and clean. To Joe it looked like the same kind of stuff he'd seen in Pat Sheehan's house, just crammed more tightly into the smaller space, and maybe cheaper and older. The kitchen was old, too, with a speckled linoleum floor, Formica countertop, and avocado green appliances. They sat at the kitchen table and Gorman produced two bottles of Rolling Rock.

"What's Art been doing since he got out of Walpole?" he asked as he slid one of the bottles across to Joe and sat down.

"He picks up a few bucks under the table driving for a limo service. Lives in couple of attic rooms over by Davis. Used to come in the Town Tavern a lot."

Gorman sat back and took a long swallow of beer. "Strange guy. I didn't know him that well, mostly just by reputation."

"What do you mean?"

"The fall he took. Not many guys volunteer for a 10 year hitch in Walpole."

"I guess not. Anything else about it that didn't make sense?"

"Everything. Art wasn't on the radar for that beef, hadn't even been questioned, no record of violence, biggest thing on his sheet was auto theft, and that was ten years before. He just walked into the station one day and said he did it. Some guys said they'd seen him in the bar that night, so that was enough. Thing was, nobody liked it. DA was pissed, wanted to pin it on Sheehan. Jerry Price, the detective on it, didn't like it, but he didn't have anything better. What's he going to do? At least it looks good on his file. And there was a lot of other shit starting to pile up."

"What do you mean?"

"That was just a couple months before all hell broke loose, the big gang war. You could smell it coming. Nobody wanted to waste time and manpower on some two-bit bar fight."

"How'd you know it was coming?"

"Shit," Gorman said disgusted. "You were a cop. You know how it works. We talked to those guys every day. I used to make it a point to drink at Tommy Haggarty's at least once a week and Riley's on another night. Between those two places, you got Pat's crowd and Hal Porter's and Jackie Albano. You could pretty much cover the bases. So, you hear things. You know when the pot's about to boil. I would have put money on it."

"So what else happened back then that Art might have got into?"

"That's the thing. We hardly ever heard of him before that. He was a hanger-on, not in on anything big. Pat had his muscle boys, but Art wasn't one of them. Only reason he was as close to Pat as he was, they went to high school together. Best we could tell, Pat let him handle some of the old established bookies. It was mostly just carrying money and slips around, but Pat needed somebody he could trust."

78

"Doesn't sound like that would get him into anything heavy."

"No way. That was a sleepy little franchise. We didn't bother them unless we got some kind of complaint."

"I still think it was something from back then. What's still open?"

"Well, of course, the ugliest one was Bobby Coluccio."

"I've heard that name. What happened to him?"

"Got hacked to pieces in his own home. Thing that made it so ugly was his kids got the same treatment – a boy about 10 and a little girl 8. I saw the pictures and I'll never get them out of my head."

"Doesn't sound like mob business. They don't usually take it out on the kids."

"No, but we couldn't come up with anything else. Coluccio was connected. He worked for Jackie, although we could never get exactly what it was he did. Jackie thought it must have been Pat Sheehan or Hal Porter that ordered it, but there wasn't anything we ever found that pointed that way."

"When was it?"

"About six months before the war started, so say September, October 1980. You could look it up."

"Okay, what else?"

"A couple months before, some woman got raped over by Union Square."

"She lived to tell about it?"

"Yeah, but just barely. Cut up pretty bad. That's the only reason I remember it. She was in the hospital for a week and all scarred when she got out. Couldn't remember much. We were sure we'd get the guy when he did another, but he never did, at least, not around here. I think she said he was short and powerful. There might be something more in the file.

We tried to keep most of the details out of the papers."

"Doesn't sound like Art, anyway. Any others you can remember?"

"Let me think." Gorman leaned back in his chair and shut his eyes. "Yeah. There was one some time back then - guy in a convenience store, old guy, maybe sixty-five, seventy. Funny how that doesn't seem so old anymore."

"What happened?"

"Armed robbery. Somebody came in with a gun, forced him to hand over the cash, then shot him right through the heart as a parting gift. Didn't seem like there was any reason for it, unless the guy knew him. We never found anyone that looked good for it."

"That it?"

"Off the top of my head, yeah. I'm sure you could dig up some more if you went through the files. Nothing that would jump out at you, screaming Art Delaney, though. He wasn't into that kind of shit. Even the bar fight was a stretch. I don't see it."

Polito shook his head thoughtfully. "Me either. But there's got to be something. I'll keep looking. Anyway, thanks. Maybe I could have got some of this out of the old newspapers, but it would have taken me all day. They don't let me look at the files down at the station anymore."

"You got fucked. That whole thing was bullshit."

"They had enough to make it stick," Joe shrugged. "They didn't like me."

"It's political - who you know, whose ass you kiss."

"I wasn't very good at it."

"Doesn't make you a bad person, or a bad cop."

"No, just an ex-cop."

80

Gorman's laugh had a sharp edge of bitterness to it.

CHAPTER 14

"Joe!"

Polito was about to climb the steps to his front door. He turned and looked across Morrison to see who had called to him. A sleek, dark SUV was parked on the opposite side of the street. Eileen Merrill opened the door and stepped out.

She crossed the street and stood in front of him. "Hello," she said, somewhat awkwardly.

"Hello."

"I was in the neighborhood, so I thought I'd drop by."

"What the hell would you be doing in this neighborhood?"

"That's what I wanted to talk to you about."

"You want to come in?" It was a question, not an invitation.

"If you don't mind. It's cold out here."

"Alright."

Joe used his key on the front door and led her up the narrow stairs to his apartment. He noticed a small piece of dead leaf on the stairs and some nicks on the banister. He felt a surge of embarrassment at the small imperfections of the house and it filled him with a teeth-grinding rage because he knew he was seeing it through her eyes. It was his house; he took pride in keeping it clean and in good repair, but it could never compete with that mansion on the hill in Lexington. He felt an unreasoning anger toward her and a bitter frustration with himself. What right did she have to judge him? How could he let her have that power? Again, she had invaded his territory and made him feel small.

He showed her into the front room, which contained a small gray couch and a maroon easy chair, both inherited from his parents. His bedroom was visible through an open door, showing more hand-me-down furniture and his mother's old quilt, that he used as a cover for his bed. At least the bed was made. In fact, both rooms were neat. His book lay open, face down on a side table next to the easy chair. Some mail he planned to answer had accumulated on the tiny writing desk in the corner. Otherwise, everything seemed to be in its place, but that didn't help at all. It still looked cheap and pathetic, his life reduced to some old junk furniture in a converted attic. He took her coat and hung it, with his own, in the closet.

"Have a seat," he said, struggling to keep the frustration and anger out of his voice. "You want a drink? All I've got is beer."

"Yes," she said quickly. "A beer would be fine."

Her voice held a slight tremor of nerves. She wasn't looking around the room with disdain, as Joe had imagined. In fact, she seemed oblivious to her surroundings. Her eyes, which he had pictured as hard with arrogance, were instead soft and vulnerable, following him with a look that was loaded with hope and fear.

He went into the kitchen to get the beer, while Eileen Merrill took a seat on the couch. When he considered pouring the beer into glasses, something he would never have done for himself or his friends, his frustration erupted in an audible grunt.

"What?" she said from the other room.

Joe walked back into the room with a sheepish grin. "Nothing," he said, handing her a bottle of Budweiser and sitting in the easy chair with his own, "just grumbling at myself."

"Oh." Her blank look said she didn't know what he was talking about and had already moved on.

"Joe, I really was in the neighborhood. The police are looking into my father's disappearance. I had to come down and meet with them. I ... I wanted to talk with you about that, and some other things I learned from Jake."

"Yeah? What?"

"Art called him. Just last Friday. I guess Art asked him not to tell anyone about the call, but I managed to get it out of him."

"What did he say? Does he know where Art is?"

"No. He didn't say. All he told him was that he wouldn't be coming over to the house for awhile. I guess he wanted to let him know that he would be back eventually, just not as soon as Jake expected."

"Did he say why?"

"No, but he gave Jake the idea that he didn't have any choice. He said something about how he had to stay away, even though he didn't want to."

"Is that it?"

"Pretty much. If he told Jake anything more than that, I couldn't get it out of him, but I was able to trace the number he was calling from. It was a public phone down at South Station."

"So at least he's still here in the city."

"He was on Friday. He could have hopped on a bus or a train right after he called. Maybe that's why he called from South Station."

"Could be," Joe shrugged. "Did he just call that one time?"

"I think that's the only time he actually talked to Jake, but there were a couple calls before that from other numbers. Whoever it was hung up when Anna answered. Those could have been from him, too."

"Did you find out where they came from?"

"Both pay phones. One was in South Boston, the other near Fields Corner."

Polito laughed. "That's beautiful," he said. "Art's making his big getaway on the Red Line."

Eileen looked confused for a moment, then brightened. "That's right. I never thought of that."

"You tell the cops about these calls?"

"No. I was going to, but I didn't like the officer who was interviewing me. I didn't trust him."

"What was his name?"

"Reese" she shuddered, "Officer Reese, but he didn't seem very professional to me."

"What do you mean?"

"It seemed like he was getting a little too personal. He had this kind of slimy charm that he insisted on using – at least until he found out how much it disgusted me. Then he turned nasty, very aggressive and threatening."

"Somerville's finest. What'd he want from you – I mean besides a quick fuck?"

"Nicely put," she said dryly. "He wanted to know where Art was. I told him I wanted to know that too. That was why I filed the Missing Persons Report. He seemed to know I was holding out on him. He knew about you, too. I think he got pretty angry, although he tried to hide it. He said this was official police business, now, and that we'd have to bring him anything we found out. I don't want to have any more to do with him."

"That's alright. If he calls again, have him talk to me. I think I might enjoy that."

"Joe," she said with a worried frown, "don't get yourself in trouble over this."

"Don't worry. If I get into trouble, it won't be because of Art ... or you."

She looked at the stubborn set of his jaw and the dark seriousness of his eyes, and she laughed. "I don't know if that's very reassuring."

"I guess not," Joe said, laughing with her. "I don't think I'm a very reassuring kind of guy."

"You're wrong about that," she said with sudden seriousness. "I came to you with a problem – you, a total stranger with no reason to get involved - and I've never felt so certain that I came to the right place. I don't know how to thank you."

"Wasn't that what last night was about?"

Eileen stiffened and her face went cold. "Is that what you thought – it was my way of paying for your services?"

"I ... don't know," Joe mumbled defensively. "It was kind of quick, you know, out of nowhere. I didn't know how to take it."

She looked down at the purse in her lap, stretching the silence. When she spoke, her voice was calm and controlled, with just a hint of ice in it. "Then let me tell you how to take it, or at least how I did. What happened last night was because I wanted it to happen, and I thought you did, too. It had nothing to do with Art or what I asked you to do for me. It had to do with you and me. That's all."

Joe nodded, wondering why he was always so wrong when he was with her. "Sorry," he said sullenly.

"Was I wrong?" she said, without the ice.

"What?"

"Didn't you want it?"

"You know I did."

"Don't you want it now?"

"Jesus," Joe said, smiling and shaking his head. He stood up and gave her his hands, pulling her up to him. The bed was only a few steps away, but they barely made it.

Later, the room was dark. A streetlight threw two rectangles of ghostly light high on the wall. Joe was sleeping.

"I've got to go," Eileen said.

"Unh," Joe muttered, shifting closer to savor her soft warmth.

"I have to."

"I know."

"I remembered something from that awful policeman. It might help."

Joe propped his head on his hand, looking down at her face, indistinct in the dark, eyes like two black holes. "I'm listening."

"He asked me if one of Art's friends had died recently. He seemed to think it might have been about a month ago. I told him I had no idea, but he wouldn't leave it alone. He asked me the same thing two or three more times, in different ways, and he seemed quite certain that it was between four and six weeks ago. I finally asked him where he'd gotten that idea. That's when he suddenly became vague, said he had 'independent information' that Art's mood had gone downhill suddenly about then, and he was looking for the reason."

"That's interesting. I wonder where he got that."

"He didn't say."

"Did he talk about his investigation at all?"

"Oh yeah. When he was trying to impress me, he told me about all the work he'd done. It sounded pretty standard to me - checking the hospitals, talking to neighbors, that kind of thing. He didn't have much to tell me, and the whole point of the meeting turned out to be him trying to get at whatever you had come up with. I didn't tell him about the money or the missionary thing. I just didn't trust him.

87

"That's good. I think your instincts are good about that guy. He's too damn interested in a routine missing persons case. From now on, you should make a show of cooperating with him. You might even want to call him in a couple days, find out how he's doing. But try not to give him anything he doesn't already know. Okay?"

"Yes, but what are we going to do?"

"I got a couple places to check tomorrow," Polito glanced at the little clock on the table beside his bed. The lighted hands showed that it was a little after 1:30. "I guess I mean today."

"Oh, God. That alarm clock is going to be brutal in the morning."

"Get going; get some sleep. I'll call you tomorrow night. What time will you be home?"

"I've got nothing in the evening, so I'm going to try to get home to have dinner with Jake, say by 6:30 or 7:00."

"Good. I'll call you sometime after that."

"Okay, but I'd rather you came over so we could talk in person."

"Why?" Joe asked with a crooked smile, "is your husband still out of town?"

"No, he got back this afternoon." Her voice was flat, void of any kind of feeling.

"So what's he going to think? Why am I there?"

"You're a friend of Art's. You're helping me look for him. That's good enough."

"Won't he get suspicious if I stay late?"

Joe felt her stiffen. "If he cared enough to notice, I might care what he thinks."

"I guess," he said doubtfully.

She reached up and pulled him down on her, kissing him deeply.

CHAPTER 15

When Eileen Merrill left Officer Chad Reese at his desk that evening, he was filled with rage. He had treated her with perfect professionalism, even thrown in a couple of his best dimpled grins as a bonus. She'd been cool at first, every bit the suburban Yuppie lawyer that she was. But, instead of responding warmly to his charms, he had seen the film of disgust pass over her face, and it was clear she was treating him like something foul she'd picked up on her shoe. She did her best to disguise it, just as he did his best to refrain from jumping across the desk and pounding her face into hamburger.

Her departure did nothing to soothe him. As her heels tapped rhythmically down the hall, he kept seeing that look of disdain hiding behind her cool features until a film of red passed over his field of vision. He grabbed his jacket and raced down the back stairs to the parking lot, just in time to see her get into a sleek black Lexus SUV and pull out onto Washington Street. He followed in his own car, a black Dodge coupe with a big engine.

She led him across town on Somerville Avenue, angling right on Elm Street. When Elm shunted her onto Russell, she seemed confused, but she managed to find Davis Square, where she took College up to Morrison. Reese followed carefully, but got stuck on Morrison when she turned into a driveway and doubled back right at him. He didn't want her to see him following, so he turned quickly into a driveway and shut off his lights as if he was parking. Half a block away, Eileen pulled to the curb across the street from Polito's house.

Reese watched her get out and cross the street. She climbed the steps to the porch and rang the bell. After waiting for a full minute with no response, she rang it again, with the same result. Finally, she went back to her car, got in, and settled down to wait.

Reese didn't know what to do. He couldn't know if she had noticed him pull into the driveway, but now he was sitting there, practically under her nose. If he pulled out of the driveway, it could tip her that she'd been followed. The driveway was only one car length deep, blocked by the garage door set into the basement of the house. At any moment, the homeowner might come out and ask him what he was doing there, which would be sure to call her attention to him. He sat there trapped and stewing for several minutes.

But the homeowner did not come out. Nothing happened. Eileen Merrill continued to sit in her car, apparently waiting for someone to come back to the house where she'd rung the bell. Reese decided his position was actually a good one. If she had seen him, there was nothing he could do about it. On the other hand, if he just sat there, he might find out who she was meeting – probably Polito – or something else that could be useful. It went against his nature to sit there, but he exercised some rare discipline and did it, passing the time by imagining himself physically and sexually dominating the bitch who had so casually and arrogantly dismissed him.

The two of them sat there for almost an hour, before Joe Polito walked down the street and Eileen called out to him. Reese had never met him, but he'd found his picture in some of the old photos kicking around the station. Even in the dark, he was pretty sure it was Polito. They went into the house, and Reese waited until he saw the third floor windows glow. He backed out of the driveway and drove to a bar in Charlestown.

Successfully tailing Eileen Merrill to her meeting with Polito somewhat calmed the rage that had initiated it, but seeing Polito succeed with her where he had failed made it personal. It gave him an idea. When he got to the bar, he took a booth and made some calls on his cell phone.

The arrangements weren't that complicated, but it was his plan. He had to sell it up the chain. When they bought it, he settled back with a look of grim satisfaction and sipped his gin, looking out at the lights of the Boston skyline.

Fifteen minutes later, the cell phone went off in his pocket. It was a man he'd never met who introduced himself only as Sanders. His voice was low and husky, with a thick Boston accent. He said he could be at the bar in half an hour. Reese said that would be fine.

When the guy showed up, Reese didn't pick him out. He was short, barely over 5' 6", and skinny, not more than 140 pounds. He had medium length dark hair, dark eyes, and a sharply hooked nose. He wore tan work pants and a blue denim shirt buttoned to the throat under his heavy coat. Reese looked right past him until he walked straight back to the booth.

"Reese?" he said, but it wasn't much of a question.

"Yeah?" Reese said, surprised.

"I'm Sanders." The man sat across from him.

"Good, good. I, um ... You heard what the job is. Right?"

"Yeah, surveillance."

"That's right. Guy sticking his nose in our business. We need to know where he goes, who he sees, what he does."

"No problem. Who's the guy?"

"Joe Polito, lives over near Davis Square."

"What's he look like?"

"About 5'9", 180, early 40s, dark hair."

"That's it? A lot of guys fit that description."

"That's all I've got. I'll see if I can get you a picture in the morning."

"What's he drive?"

"I'll get you that in the morning, too."

Sanders looked sour. "We could waste a lot of time if I get on the wrong guy."

"I know, I know. I'll get you what you need."

"Where do I pick him up?"

"At his place. I saw him go in about ten. He'll probably be there in the morning. If not, he hangs out at the Town Tavern in the square."

"When do you want me on him?"

"Tomorrow morning should be good enough. How about we do this: I'll meet you at 7:00 in the Dunkin Donuts in Davis Square. I'll bring a picture and find out what he drives, get you set up."

"Fine," Sanders said flatly. "What about tomorrow night? You need him covered at night, too?"

"I don't know. Let's see how tomorrow goes. The big thing is, he's looking for an old man named Art Delaney. If he gets close, or you see the old man, I got to know immediately."

"Bring a picture of him, too."

"Yeah, okay."

"One other thing," Sanders leaned a little closer.

"Yeah?"

"I follow the guy. I pick up information and get it to you. That's all. You get what I'm saying."

"I get it. If we need to um ... do something about it. I'll make other arrangements."

"I don't even want to know about any of that. Okay?"

"No problem. If it comes to it, I might even handle it myself."

Sanders' face twisted into a grimace of distaste. "You don't get it. That's more than I want to know."

"Oh. Right," Reese backtracked quickly. "Sorry."

"I'll see you in the morning," Sanders said, sliding out of the booth. He walked away without a backward glance, and he was invisible in the crowd before he reached the door.

CHAPTER 16

Polito woke up feeling good. He had a few things planned for the day and it felt like he was making progress, even if he wasn't any closer to finding Art Delaney than he had been when he started. Eileen Merrill was part of it. One by one, she was shattering his preconceived notions of a Yuppie bitch. He couldn't remember ever being so pleased to be wrong.

He showered, shaved, brushed his teeth and dressed. He was down on the street by a quarter of eight. The air was cold and dry, with a bright blue sky overhead. He walked up to the little sandwich place by the rotary and had his coffee, eggs and toast with the *Globe*.

There were a lot of people out - people waiting at the bus stop, people walking up and down College Ave, people walking through the little park on the hill across the street. Joe didn't notice a skinny little man with a hook nose who strolled up College about a block behind him and went into the park when Joe went into the sandwich shop. The man found a bench that overlooked the shop where he sat in the brisk morning sunshine while Joe had his breakfast. He too had a copy of the *Globe*, and he opened the sports section, but didn't read much. Every 15 or 20 seconds, he would glance up at the door of the sandwich shop. With his attention so divided, it took him ten minutes to get through a preview of the Bruins' next game. It was cold and boring, sitting on the park bench, waiting for Polito to come out of the sandwich shop, but Sanders was patient and dressed for it.

Joe took his time over coffee, reading the sports page and the metro section, then glancing briefly at the obituaries to get an idea of the format. When he left the shop and walked down to the square, he didn't notice the little man get up, leave his paper on the bench and leisurely stroll after him. Joe went into the Red Line station and down the stairs to the platform. An inbound train rolled in a couple minutes later and he got on. Sanders got on the next car.

It was mid-morning, well past the morning rush. The T wasn't crowded, and Joe got a seat. When he rode the subway, Joe had a bad habit of looking a little too closely at the other riders. It had nearly gotten him into a fight on more than one occasion. That morning, no one seemed to mind Joe's attention. They were mostly student types, with their down parkas, their fleece, and their salt-stained shoes. Even the older ones looked like students. Some had long hair, as if they had never left the hippie era. They all swayed synchronously with the motion of the train as it rolled through the tunnel.

When Polito got off at the Kendall/MIT stop, Sanders did too. Joe walked north from the station on a wide pedestrian walk lined with young, leafless trees on one side, giant office buildings on the other. Everything looked neat and prosperous. Some of the people going into the buildings wore suits. The tall buildings gleamed in the bright blue sky. It looked nothing like the blighted and torn up old section of city he'd seen when he rode his bike there thirty years earlier. He walked past the Cambridge Police Station and saw a dozen uniformed officers passing in and out of the front door. When he turned and walked up the side street that ran along the building, there were a dozen more going in and out of side doors to their cruisers parked along the street.

The station took up almost the whole block. When Joe got near the end of it, he saw that the street came to a T, which meant the address he was looking for had to be back in the direction he had come from. So, he turned and doubled back. Sanders had already turned the corner and started down the street when he saw Polito turn and head right at him. He couldn't turn and double back himself, and he didn't particularly want to pass Polito face to face, so he cut across the street at an angle, to walk on the other side where Joe would be less likely to notice him.

"Hey," a cop yelled from a small group standing around a cruiser, "use the crosswalk, for crying out loud. At least in front of the station. Let's show a little respect." His buddies laughed.

Sanders hurried across the street and Joe looked over at him with some sympathy. The cop was just busting his balls, making a joke at his expense, and there was nothing he could do about it. He was just a quiet little guy with a big nose, and they were cops. He must be bullshit. Polito could imagine that happening to him, and he knew he wouldn't have the good sense to turn away and just keep walking like the little man. He'd probably go over and give the cops some lip, get himself in trouble. He needed to learn from guys like that, guys who could walk away from trouble.

On the next block, he found the address he was looking for on a small faded sign above a steel door in a dirty cement block building. At the corner of the building, there was a gated driveway leading into a cramped lot where half a dozen black Chryslers sat parked. The gate was open and Polito went through. Just inside the gate, he entered the building through another metal door, this one dented and corroded, with a plastic sign that said "Employees Only." The room he entered was small and divided in half by a chest high counter. A film of greasy dust lay over the walls and floor.

Behind the counter, a fat man was molded into a padded swivel chair on rollers. He had dark hair, dark eyes, dark stubble. His clothes were various shades of dirty gray, as if he was covered by the same greasy dust that had settled over everything else. He sat beside a small desk, where loose leaf notebooks and papers with greasy smudges surrounded a large telephone console with multiple displays and rows of buttons. Narrow strips of chrome around the displays and buttons seemed to be the only shiny surfaces in the whole room. The fat man was reading a tabloid newspaper. He glanced up for only a moment when Joe came in.

His eyes returned to the paper and he said, "Sign says 'Employees Only. What do you want? We're not hiring."

"I'm not looking for a job," Polito said. "I'm looking for a friend of mine – Art Delaney. I know he works for a limo service out of Kendall. This the one?"

The man looked up without curiosity. "Why should I tell you? You a cop? An inspector?"

"Neither, just a friend. Art's been missing for over a week. His family's worried." Polito pulled a hundred dollar bill out of his pocket and held it where the fat man could see it. "And why you should tell me – is this a good enough reason."

"That'll work." Without getting out of it, the man shuffled his chair over to the counter and pulled the bill from between Joe's fingers. He turned it over and examined it carefully, then put it into the pocket of his greasy pants. Finally, he looked up at Joe with a challenging sneer.

"We got no Delaney working here. I never heard of the guy. And you don't get your money back."

"I don't want it. If that's the truth, you earned it. If it's not, I'll come back and take it out of your fat face."

Under the grease, the man's face turned an unhealthy shade of purple. He began edging his chair away from the counter. "That's the truth," he said, "but it's too bad. I'd love the chance to kick your ass."

"I'm right here," Joe said.

The man glared across the counter at him. Joe could see the wheels moving slowly and uncertainly behind his eyes. "Get the fuck out of here," he finally said, "and thanks for the hundred."

"Like I said, if you told me the truth, you earned it. If not, I'll be back." Polito turned and walked out the door.

At the next place, a few blocks away, the office and dispatcher were cleaner, but this one didn't see any more reason to cooperate than the first. He was a dapper man of about 60, with white hair and a thick white mustache. He wore a quilted vest to ward off the chill in his tiny office, but there was no sign warning the pubic to keep out. In fact, he smiled and seemed glad to see Polito, until he found out what he wanted.

"We don't give out information on our employees unless it is legally required," he frowned apologetically.

"So Art is one of your employees."

"I didn't say that."

"Listen," Joe said, bringing out another hundred. "I'm not trying to get you or Art in a jam. I'm just helping his family find him. They'd be very grateful for anything you can tell me."

The money did its magic. The man glanced at it with some interest and ran a finger over the thatch on his upper lip. "The family, huh? Who? What family?"

"His daughter and grandson."

The man raised bright blue eyes to frankly search Polito's face. "What's the grandson's name?"

"Jake."

The man smiled and took the bill. "Art always talks about that kid. What do you want to know?"

"When was the last time you saw Art?"

"Weekend before last. He did a few airport runs and took some guy and his date around for a night on the town."

"What night was that?"

"Saturday."

"Heard from him since?"

"As a matter of fact, he called a couple days ago."

"What about?"

"Wanted to get his money. Also, looking for work."

"Did you give him the money?"

"No, I told him he could have half a day tomorrow, and he said he'd pick it up then."

"Tomorrow. He tell you where to get in touch with him in the mean time?"

"No. Said he'd call in the morning to see what time he should come in. It kind of depends on how much we've got booked."

"Where does he pick up the car?"

"Right here."

"Morning, afternoon, evening – got any idea?"

"He's on for the evening, for sure. If it's busy, I'll have him come in some time in the afternoon."

"Alright," Joe said, grabbing a small pad of paper and a pen, scribbling his name and number. "When he calls, tell him I want to talk to him. Tell him Eileen and Jake are worried. Have him give me a call at that number – Joe Polito. He knows me, knows I wouldn't fuck him over."

"What if he doesn't want to talk to you?"

"If he says that, then you call me. In fact, call me anyway. Tell me what he says. Art's not thinking too clearly right now. He might not know what's best for him. You want to help him out, call me. I'm on his side."

"I might do that," the man said with a wry smile, "but I'd be sure to if there's any more of that incentive money available."

"There is," Joe said immediately. "You keep me informed about what's happening with Art, there's another one of those nice crisp bills waiting for you."

"In that case, you'll definitely hear from me."

"Good. There's one other thing, and it's worth money, too."

"I'm listening."

"Someone else may come around asking about Art. I don't know what their game is, but I think Art would be better off if they don't find him. If you can hold them off, give them as little as possible, I'd appreciate it."

"Appreciate it," the man repeated as if he liked the feel of the words on his tongue. "Would you appreciate it as much as you appreciated the information I gave you today?"

"Maybe more."

CHAPTER 17

Polito walked to Union Square. It was about a mile and a half, but the sidewalks were clear and the sunshine was pleasant. When he arrived at the Somerville Police Station just after 11:00, he went to the front desk and asked for Officer Reese.

The uniformed officer seated behind the desk was young, in his early twenties. He had short blond hair and innocent blue eyes that he tried to offset with heavy muscles in his arms and chest and a flat stare. "I'll see if he's here," he responded, without enthusiasm, punching buttons on his console.

He held the phone to his ear for a minute, put it back on the console, and shook his head. "Not in."

"Alright. I'll leave a message."

The blond kid continued to stare at him without expression.

"Don't you want a piece of paper and a pencil to take it down?"

The kid's doughy white face turned pink, but he reached out and positioned a message pad in front of him on the desk. He picked up a pen that was sitting beside it and waited silently.

"Tell him Joe Polito stopped by. If he wants to talk, have him call me at 617-724-4463."

The kid scribbled, but did not look up.

"You got that," Polito said, "or was I going too fast for you."

When the kid finally looked at him, his face was mottled red and white, and his baby blue eyes narrowed with hate. "Get the fuck out of here," he whispered hoarsely.

Joe cupped his hand behind his ear. "Beg your pardon?" he said as if he hadn't heard.

The kid started to get out of his chair, then thought better of it and sank back. His hateful glare never left Polito's face. "You heard me. Get out," the kid muttered through gritted teeth, "unless you want to get arrested."

"Huh," Joe said, grinning in the kid's face. "I didn't know it was illegal to ask a cop to do his job."

The kid said nothing, just glared through the bullet-proof glass.

"Well, I've certainly enjoyed our little chat. Have a nice day." Joe turned and walked out the door.

Polito walked through Union Square, marveling at the number of Brazilian businesses, storefronts with signs in Portuguese that barely bothered to translate their message into English. Some of the guys he worked with doing roofing came from this neighborhood. They knew enough English to get by, and they worked hard. They got paid cash under the table, and some of them were probably illegal, but Joe had no desire to send them back. They were doing what generations of Somervillains had done before, what his own grandparents had done. They came here to work and make a better life for themselves and their families. As he saw it, that was what the city was for, part of its fundamental nature, and something to be proud of. The Brazilians didn't organize massive criminal businesses to bleed the city dry, as the Irish and Italians had done, and they weren't Yuppie colonists taking over in the name of Starbucks and sushi. But he feared for them, just as he feared for himself and the rest of his old time working class neighbors. Slowly, but inevitably, they were losing their grip on the city. Economic forces and changing tastes were forcing them out. The Brazilians would find someplace to go, someplace with cheap housing and jobs, someplace where enough of them could gather to feel comfortable, a new home. For Joe, it wouldn't be that easy. Somerville was his home. For him, there would be no other, not in this lifetime. If he went somewhere else – anywhere - he'd be a stranger. The only thing he could do was hold onto his home as long as he could, until it changed so much it was no longer home.

From the square, he walked up Prospect Hill, heading for the Main Branch of the Somerville Public Library. It was a short walk that happened to take him within half a block of Pat Sheehan's place. He made a detour onto Munroe and walked past the big house that looked down on him through the bare branches of trees in the front yard. It was a beautiful old home, well over a hundred years old, with four brick chimneys poking through the slate roof. It must have been built to house one of Somerville's leading citizens. Wryly, Joe had to admit that Pat Sheehan fit that description. There was a time when a few cents of every dollar collected by the city's loan sharks, bookies, drug dealers and pimps went to him. Now the house was waiting for him to die, waiting for a new elite to take over. Joe thought bitterly that it would probably be some radiologist from Marblehead eager to experience the trendy urban lifestyle. He saw that as going from bad to worse, but the house didn't care. There were no signs of life behind the windows that impassively reflected the sky.

At the library, Joe went straight to the front desk. A white-haired woman in glasses and a green sack dress was scanning returned books into the library's computer. When Joe stopped in front of her desk, she looked up and smiled.

"May I help you?"

"Yes," Joe said. "I need to look at some old issues of the *Globe*. Do you have them?"

"Yes, of course. How old?"

"Well, I'd like to look at all the issues from a four week period starting about 7 weeks ago."

"Oh, that's no problem, but if there's something particular you're looking for, we could do a search."

"That'd be too easy," Joe grinned. "The problem is, I don't really know what I'm looking for. I'm hoping I'll know it when I see it."

"In that case, you should go over to the reference desk and talk to Miss Pelletier. She can set you up with a viewer."

"Great. Thank you."

"You're welcome."

Miss Pelletier was just as helpful, and she soon had Joe seated at a computer screen, paging through a month's worth of deaths as documented in the *Globe's* obituaries.

In his quick look at the obits pages in that morning's *Globe*, Joe had seen that there were three main types: there were the basic death notices that said when a person was born, who their relatives were and something about funeral and memorial services; there were bigger pieces that must have been sponsored by relatives, giving, in addition to the standard notice, some sense of the dead person's accomplishments; and finally, there were similar biographical stories of the famous or near famous, included for their news value.

Joe glanced through the basic death notices, by far the most numerous of the three types. He tried to concentrate on Irish names, looking for anyone related to a Delaney. He found a woman who had died in her ninety-ninth year named O'Hair. She was survived by a niece living in Huntington Beach California, whose married name was Delaney. It seemed unlikely that this connection could have made much of an impression on Art, if it was, in fact, any connection at all. Joe kept looking.

He spent a little more time on the longer, biographical obituaries, thinking that some connection could exist in the body of one of these stories. It was slow going. It took him over two hours to make it through the first three weeks, and he was thinking that the whole thing was a waste of time, when he came across the sad story of Betty Coluccio's life and death in the *Globe* of Monday, January 24.

The article was an unusual format. It wasn't subsidized by any of her relatives, and Betty Coluccio was not a public figure. She had played a peripheral part in an event of historical infamy, but her role was that of a secondary victim, and the event had occurred long ago. The enterprising obit writer had dredged up the awful history in order to fill out a short column that he probably thought would put a period to her life and the event that shattered it. Joe didn't think so. He was pretty sure that Betty Coluccio's death was not the end of the story.

Betty Coluccio (nee Riordan) was born January 16, 1949, in South Boston. She went to South Boston High and graduated in 1967. In 1968, she married Robert (Bobby) Coluccio, and quickly had two children, Bobby Jr. in 1970, and Anna in 1972. The family originally lived in Dorchester, but moved to Somerville in 1978. Bobby Sr. worked occasionally as a truck driver, delivering produce from the Chelsea Market. He was also alleged to be involved with organized crime, with a record of relatively minor criminal offenses dating back to his teenage years. In 1980, his career came to a sudden end when he and his two children were stabbed to death in their home in the Winter Hill section of Somerville. On the night of the murders, Betty Coluccio had made her weekly visit to her mother's home in Dorchester. Usually, she brought the two children with her, but that night she left them home so that she could go out for a drink with an old high school friend after seeing her mother. When she got home, she found her husband and her two children dead in a scene of unimaginable blood and horror. Their murder was never solved, but police believed it to be mob-related. It helped to ignite the Somerville gang war that lasted nearly five years and claimed at least three dozen lives.

Betty Coluccio had been a normal, happy young woman, but the discovery of her murdered family was a shock from which she never recovered. Police said that the murder scene was the most gruesome any of them had ever encountered. For the wife and mother of the victims, the shock of discovering that scene was compounded with her guilt for having left the children home that evening, a casual decision that led directly to their deaths. The weight of it all was too much for her emotional balance. She was hospitalized briefly following the discovery of the bodies, but there seemed to be nothing the doctors could do. She spent the rest of her life, another 30 years, a hopeless alcoholic and drug addict, wandering the streets of Somerville, running from the memories that haunted her. When her body was found in an abandoned building, she had been dead for more than a week. No one reported her missing. All her family and friends had either died or fallen away over the years, leaving no one to wonder what had become of her. Police investigators saw no evidence of foul play or drug overdose. Noting that temperatures during the week in which she died had fallen as low as 10 degrees Fahrenheit, they were looking into the possibility that she simply froze to death. She was buried alongside her husband and children.

Joe didn't look any further. He believed he had what he had come for. He shut down his terminal, thanked Miss Pelletier, and left the library. Out front, on Highland Avenue, he waited for the bus to Davis Square. It would have been a long walk, and he was getting hungry.

While Polito waited, Sanders called Reese. "He's getting on a bus and I can't follow. Looks like he's heading back to Davis.... No, he saw me this morning.... An accident. Shit happens.... No, if he sees me again he might put it together and realize he's being tailed.... Yeah, okay. I'll check it out. If I lose him, I'll call you.... Now?... Alright, here it is: had breakfast at a sandwich shop near the Powder House Rotary; took the T to Kendall and walked around by the Cambridge Police Station. That's where he saw me. I had to back off, and I lost him for a few minutes. When I picked him up again, he walked to the Somerville Police Station and went in for a couple minutes. From there, he walked to the Library up on Highland. He spent two hours on one of the library computers.... No, I couldn't get close enough. Now he's waiting for the bus on Highland.... Yeah, okay. Anything, so long as I don't have to walk. You got a number for a cab company?..."

Sanders' cab picked him up just before Joe's bus arrived.

CHAPTER 18

When he got off in Davis Square, Joe didn't see Sanders, who was standing about half a block from the bus stop. Joe went around the corner to the Town Tavern, where he had a late lunch and read his book. At three o'clock, he got up and nodded at Tim as he left.

From the tavern, he walked to Art's place on Elston. Art's mailbox had a new load of junk mail. Joe took it upstairs, knocking on Lisa Landry's door as he passed through the landing. There was no response, so he went on up to Art's apartment. He spent 10 minutes going through the mail and the apartment, learning nothing. He left the door to the stairwell open, sat down in Art's only comfortable chair and pulled out his book.

This time, he read only a few pages before he heard the sound of someone coming up the stairs. He stuffed the book back into the pocket of his sweatshirt, closed up the apartment, and went down the stairs, where he found Lisa Landry unlocking her apartment door.

She was wearing her light green scrubs, and she carried an enormous black leather purse with enough silver buckles, zippers and studs to satisfy a Hell's Angel. A cigarette dangling from her lips sent a jagged plume of smoke up to the ceiling. The stairs squawked and squealed under him as Joe came down, causing her to turn startled eyes toward him.

"Oh. You," she said without much feeling one way or the other.

"Yup, me," Joe said brightly. "Still looking for Art. You hear anything?"

"Not a word." She opened the door, giving him her characteristic squint through the smoke of her cigarette. "You want a beer? I'll tell you all about it."

"Doesn't sound like there's much to tell, but I could use a beer."

He followed her into the messy kitchen and took his place at the table. Not much had changed since the last time he'd been there. The same dirty dishes were stacked chaotically on the counters. The same garbage was still piled in the corner. The ash tray on the table must have been emptied. It was no longer overflowing with butts, though it was well on its way with a new load.

Lisa dropped her purse on the counter. "For a quiet old man, that guy gets more attention than a god damn movie star," she said.

"Why?" Joe asked. "Did someone else come looking for him?"

"A cop. Showed up a little after you left on Wednesday."

"A cop named Reese?"

"That's the one," she said sourly. "You know him?"

"No, but we seem to be covering the same ground. I've been hearing a lot about him."

"Nothing good, I hope."

"You didn't like him?"

"Let's just say he left a bad taste in my mouth."

"Actually, that makes it unanimous. Nobody I talked to seemed to like him."

"He's a fucking asshole," she said bluntly. "Thinks he's hot shit. I don't go for that."

"Who does?" Joe agreed. "What'd he want?"

"Looking for old Mr. Delaney."

"So you told him what you told me?"

"Right."

"He ask you anything about Art getting upset over someone who died?"

"Oh," she said quickly. "No ... um, that was me. After you left, I remembered I went upstairs one night and the old man was all upset about something, babbling on about God and forgiveness and stuff. I told that asshole cop he might have been upset because someone died. He had the *Globe* open to the obituaries page, right there on the table."

"You remember when that happened, what the date was?"

Lisa shook her head. "No. About a month ago. I don't ... No, wait. It was a Monday. I was back on morning shift, so I needed to get to sleep early. I went up to have a couple beers with him, you know, help me relax."

"Any idea which Monday that would have been?"

"Maybe the end of January," she said doubtfully. "I'm just guessing."

"That's okay. What'd Reese think about it?"

"He didn't say. Mostly, he just wanted to know what was bothering him."

"What'd you tell him?"

"I had no idea; Art wouldn't say. Then he wanted to know if there was anybody else Art might have talked to about it – you know, a priest, the cops, friends. I couldn't help him there, either."

"You tell him about me?"

"Um, yeah. I mean, he's a cop, right?"

"Right," Joe said, absently. "The thing I'm wondering about is that Sunday. He woke you up the night before, coming in late. It seems like he left the next morning, Sunday morning, and never came back. I'm wondering if anyone saw him leave."

"I didn't. Like I said, I had the morning shift, so I didn't get home until late afternoon."

"Oh yeah, right. But maybe you can tell me this: Art went to mass that Sunday. Was that his normal routine? Mass every Sunday?"

"I think so. I mean, I don't know if it was every Sunday, but it seemed like he was pretty regular."

"What did he wear?"

She smiled. "Always wore a suit. In fact, always the same old dark gray suit. I don't think he had any other."

"Do you know if he usually went somewhere after mass?"

"I don't know. I don't think so."

"What about transportation. How did he get there?"

"Took his car. Only time that old heap ever moved, as far as I know. Art didn't like driving. Going as far as St. Clements was about all he could manage."

"Is Art's car one of the ones in the driveway?"

"Yeah, the old Ford. Other one belongs to Mr. Mullins on the first floor. I was the last one into the building, so I get to park on the street."

"But you don't know if Art took his car that Sunday?"

"No. You could ask Mr. Mullins."

"I think I will. What I really want is to find someone who saw him that morning, either coming or going."

"You should be talking to Mrs. Wilkins across the street. She's our one-woman neighborhood watch."

"Really?"

"Oh, yeah," she laughed. "Every time I have some guy over, she's right on top of it, making some kind of wisecrack. She's about 90, but she doesn't miss a thing."

"Perfect. You say she's right across the street?"

"Right."

"If I went over there, you think she'd talk to me?"

Lisa frowned. "I don't know. She's a little paranoid. I think that's why she watches the street all day."

"Maybe if you came over with me ..."

"Sure," she shrugged. "Why not. Give her something to talk about for the next week or two."

Mrs. Wilkins was tall and thin, with white hair. Despite her age, she carried herself perfectly erect, and her eyes were clear and apparently quite sharp. She gave Lisa a tight-lipped wry smile and frankly examined Joe.

"Hello, Lisa," she said. "I see you've brought your friend out in the daylight. Usually they try to sneak in and out in the dark, like vampires."

"Well, they don't get past you, do they?" Lisa laughed. "Mrs. Wilkins, this is Joe Polito. He's a friend of Art Delaney." She pointed back across the street at her house. "You know, on the third floor."

"I know Art. Hello, Mr. Polito," she said holding out a dry withered hand.

Joe held it briefly. "Hello, Mrs. Wilkins. I'm trying to find Art. I don't know if you've noticed he hasn't been here for awhile."

"Oh, yes. I've been wondering about that myself. I hope he's alright."

"I do too. His family is concerned. They asked me to look for him, and I've got a couple questions I'd like to ask you that might help."

"Alright. Why don't you come into the porch, here? It's a little chilly to be standing outside."

"Thank you."

Joe stepped into the glassed in porch that was only a few degrees warmer than the street. Lisa went back down the steps and lit a cigarette. Mrs. Wilkins sat on one of the wicker porch chairs and Joe took the other.

"Please don't think anything of my nasty comment about Lisa's men friends," Mrs. Wilkins said. "It's a bad habit of mine – making judgments. Too much time on my hands. Lisa is really a very nice girl. She's just lonely since she finally got rid of her no good husband. I hope you won't think any less of her because of what I said."

"I don't. To me, it sounded like some good-natured kidding between neighbors."

"That's right, but there's a time and a place for it, and sometimes my judgment isn't very good about that. Now, what did you want to know about Art Delaney?"

"I guess the first thing is to figure out when Art left home. From what I've gathered so far, I think it was a week ago last Sunday. What do you think?"

"Well, all I know is, that's the last time I saw him."

"So you did see him that day."

"Yes. He went to mass, as he always does."

"How did he get there?"

"That was the odd thing. Normally, he takes his car. But this time, a cab came by and picked him up."

"Really. You didn't happen to see him come back, did you?"

"Of course I did. A big black car dropped him off, right in front of his house and waited for him. Two minutes later, he came down and got back in the car. The car drove away, and that's the last I saw of him."

"Did he have anything with him when he left?"

"Yes. He was carrying a brown paper shopping bag."

Joe nodded. "Can you tell me anything about the car or the driver?"

"I can't tell you very much about the car. It was big and black, probably American made. I think the driver was an old man. It was a little hard to tell, because of the light reflecting off the car windows, but I'm fairly certain he had white hair. It seemed to be quite thin, too, as if he was going bald."

"Thank you. That's very helpful. Just one more question: Was there anyone else in the car?"

"No," she said with certainty, "not unless they were ducking down below the windows."

"Okay, great. I really appreciate your help, Mrs. Wilkins."

"Well, I'm just glad I could be useful. Sometimes people aren't so pleased to have a Nosey Parker like me on the street, but I think it's always good to be aware of what's going on around you. It keeps us all safer. In fact, there is one more thing I saw that you may want to be aware of."

"What's that?" Joe asked.

"After you went into Lisa's house a little while ago, I saw a man walk down the street. He only glanced up at the house, so I didn't think anything of it. But then he walked by in the other direction about 10 minutes later, again with a casual glance up at the house. I wonder if he has anything to do with your investigation."

"Huh. I wonder too. What did he look like?"

"He was a small man, no more than 5'6" I would say, and probably thin, though it was hard to tell because of the long gray overcoat he wore. He had a small face, with a big hook nose. His eyes were dark, and he wore a narrow brim hat. Is that someone you know?"

"No," Joe said slowly. Something in her description seemed familiar, but he couldn't think where he'd met such a person. "But I'll keep an eye out for him, now. Thanks again."

"You're quite welcome. I hope you find Mr. Delaney. It was nice to meet you."

"It was nice to meet you, too, Mrs. Wilkins."

Joe crossed the street with Lisa and stood in front of her house. He was distracted by what he'd learned and eager to follow up on it. Mrs. Wilkins' description of the little man with the big nose still bothered him. An image swam around in his head just out of reach of consciousness.

"Thanks, Lisa. That was more help than you know."

"Do you think it will lead you to the old man?"

"Sooner or later. All I've got now is a bunch of guesses, but they're getting stronger with every little thing I pick up. What I got from Mrs. Wilkins gives me a couple new leads to work, and I wouldn't have got them without your help."

"Oh, that was nothing," she said with a sigh of resignation. "So I guess you've got to go work your case, then. No time to come up for another beer, huh?"

"Not right now, Lisa. I've got to go. I'll catch you another time, okay?"

"Right."

She trudged up the steps and pushed aside the rotting front door of her building. Joe glanced back, as she disappeared inside. His eyes were shadowed by a troubled frown.

CHAPTER 19

Before he reached the end of the street, Joe was on his cell phone to Pat Sheehan. Rose answered and said that Pat was taking a nap. Could he call back in an hour? Joe said he would and went back to the Town Tavern.

He got another beer at the bar and took it to his table. The afternoon crowd was starting to fill in, but the conversations were subdued. Joe had just opened his book when the phone in his pocket rang loudly enough for everyone to hear. Joe heard it too, but he didn't get many calls. It took him a second ring before he realized where the odd annoying chirp was coming from. He fumbled in his pocket and got it in the middle of the fourth ring.

"Yeah," he said.

"This Joe Polito?" someone asked – a voice Joe could not place.

"Yes."

"This is Al Trautman at Luxury Limo."

"Oh, yeah. Did you hear from Art?"

"No, but I heard something about him. I thought you might want to know."

"Absolutely."

"And I'm sure you'll show your appreciation like you did this morning."

"Of course."

"Okay. After you left, I looked at the bookings sheet for tomorrow night. Art was already assigned to a booking. I thought that was odd."

"Why? You said he was working tomorrow night."

"Right, but we don't usually assign drivers to specific bookings ahead of time, unless they're specifically requested. Helps us manage the drivers."

"You mean someone requested Art by name?"

"That's right. I knew I didn't make the assignment, so I called up my other dispatcher. He remembered taking that booking because it seemed kind of odd to him, too."

"Don't people often ask for a particular driver?"

"It happens, but not too often. The thing that made it strange was that the client asked what nights Art was working before he booked it. When my dispatcher told him Art was only working tomorrow night, the guy said that was perfect and he booked it."

"That does sound weird. When did he take that call?"

"Last night, late."

"Who was this guy?"

"He said he was booking it for his boss, David Trudell, and he used a credit card under that name to hold it."

"Where is Art supposed to pick him up?"

"The Parker House, 8:30."

"Okay, good. Call me again when you talk to Art."

"Sure. And you'll stop by and deliver your appreciation?"

"I'll see you tomorrow."

"I'm looking forward to it."

At five, the tavern was busy. There was too much noise to make a call. Joe walked up the street to the horrible six-way intersection at the heart of Davis Square.

Waiting for the light, he looked up College and saw two cops standing in front of a convenience store. One of them said something and the other laughed. That was all it took to jog loose the memory of the cops busting the balls of the jaywalker by the Cambridge Police Station. That was why Mrs.

Wilkins' description rang a bell. She was describing the jaywalker. Could it be a coincidence? Joe scanned the image in his brain – the gray coat, the narrow brim hat, the height, the nose. It was all there, too much for coincidence.

Joe crossed the street, sat on a bench in the square and dialed Sheehan's number. Rose answered and went to get him.

"Yeah, what do you want, Polito?" Sheehan rasped into the phone.

"Some answers. You didn't tell me much the last time we talked, and half of that was bullshit."

"Fuck you. I don't owe you anything. I'll tell you whatever I want."

"No, you don't owe me anything, but you do owe Art something – a lot, I think – and if you want to help him, you'll help me."

"God damn it, that's what I keep telling you. You can't help Art, and everything you're doing is just going to bring down a shitstorm on him and on you."

"Why is that? The Coluccio killings still that hot?"

There was perfect silence on the line for almost a minute. Joe waited, fairly certain he'd hit the mark.

"We got to talk." Sheehan's voice was low and hoarse, but urgent.

"That's what I've been saying – talk, straight, no bullshit."

"Yeah, yeah. When can you get your ass over here?"

"Twenty minutes, but there's a complication. I think somebody's tailing me. It wouldn't be one of yours, would it?"

"No, god damn it, but that's the shit I've been telling you about."

"Alright, but what do you want me to do about it? Is it okay if they follow me to your place?"

"No, that would be a problem. Can you lose him?"

"I think so. He's been following me all day, but now that I know he's there and what he looks like – I think so."

"Make sure you do."

There are two entrances to the Davis Square Red Line station. One was directly across College Avenue from Joe's bench. The other was half a block away across the square on Holland. They connect through a pedestrian tunnel running under the square. Joe crossed to the Holland Street entrance and went in. The evening rush was in full swing, a constant stream of people filing in and out. Joe went straight through the little covered entry, past the stairs and escalator that led down to the subway station, and out through another set of doors to the bike path in back. From there, he turned left down a small side street. Pausing at the intersection of one of the streets that ran off the square, he looked around the corner of a building to see if he could spot the little man. He wasn't there, but that didn't mean he wasn't on the tail. If he was good, he would have used the other entrance, and picked Joe up again underground. Joe hustled across the street and ran along the narrow walk behind one of the new buildings that had just gone up in the square. Along the far side of the building, another cross street ran into the square. Again, Joe peered around the corner of the building, and again, could not see the man with the big nose. There was a taxi stand at the corner, with two cabs sitting there. Joe ran up and jumped in the first cab in line.

"Union Square," he said. "Quick."

The driver pulled forward to the light, where the street flowed into the square. Joe stared out through the windshield, searching for the man who had evidently followed him all day. Just as the cab pulled into the intersection, the man came out of the subway entrance on College. Through the crowd, Joe caught a glimpse that took in the coat, the hat, the nose. It was the jaywalker and the man Mrs. Wilkins had described. He stood on the sidewalk, casually scanning the square, as if looking for a ride that was supposed to pick him up. He didn't see Joe in the cab that turned down Elm and was quickly out of sight.

CHAPTER 20

Joe was angry. It made no sense, but he was angry at the little man for following him. He was angry at himself for not spotting him sooner. Most of all, he was angry that he still did not know who was behind it, or why. He wanted to go back to Davis, wrap his hands around that scrawny neck and squeeze until the man coughed up who he was working for. Instead, he swallowed his anger and swore it wouldn't happen again.

With that in mind, he did not go directly to Pat Sheehan's place. He got out of the cab in Union Square to complicate his trail, just in case. As he walked up the hill, he doubled back and made a quick loop, watching closely for any signs of a follower. Maybe the guy had a partner. Maybe he managed to get back on the tail somehow. By the time he went up the walk to Sheehan's front door, he was certain no one had managed to tail him there.

Rose let him in, but she was angry, too. "What did you say to him?" she demanded in a harsh whisper. "He's all upset."

"It's not what I said," Joe whispered back. "It's just the past catching up with him."

Rose shook her head with bitter resignation. "He hasn't got that long. Why can't he have some peace?"

Joe had some ideas about that, but it wasn't a question, so he kept his mouth shut.

Rose led him into the same stuffy parlor where he had talked with Pat Sheehan the day before. Sheehan sat slumped in a stuffed chair, glaring at him as they came in. Anger brought color to his cheeks, but against his pale gray complexion, the color was ghastly, like an undertaker's makeup on a corpse. Rose said nothing. She turned and left Joe standing just inside the room, closing the door softly behind him.

"Now I know why they bounced you out of Somerville PD," Sheehan said. "You're too god damn smart and too god damn stubborn. Tell me what you know."

Joe sat on the sofa. "I know a bunch of things I didn't know yesterday. I know Art's alive. I know it was the death of Bobby Coluccio's widow that set off his attack of conscience. I know somebody's interested enough to have me followed. And I know you were the one that helped him disappear. I don't know how it all fits together - but I bet you do."

"So what?" Sheehan grumbled. "It wouldn't do you any good if I told you – just get you killed, probably. And Art."

"Then tell me this - no bullshit: Is it you that's having me followed?"

Sheehan studied him, as if trying to read something in Polito's face. "Why would I do that?"

"I can think of a couple possible reasons," Joe said mildly. "But let's just go with the obvious. You're trying to keep the lid on Art. If I find him, he might open up about an old murder that's still too hot to talk about. You want to know if I'm getting close. How's that?"

"Makes sense," Sheehan nodded, "but it's not me. Anyway, why should I bother having you followed? If I want to know how you're doing finding Art, all I've got to do is wait until you come and tell me."

"That's true, but maybe you don't trust me to tell you everything."

"You're right; I don't, but it's still not me."

"But you know who it is, don't you?"

Sheehan frowned. "I could guess."

"Then tell me. Whoever's having me followed knows what I'm doing. If they're as dangerous as you say, they might decide to kill me just for looking. It'd be nice to know who they are and what they're afraid of, so I could protect myself."

"You can't protect yourself." Sheehan's voice was scornful, but exhausted. "Even I couldn't do that. I've got ten guys I could call up who'd go to war with me, guys who know how it's done. We'd all be dead within a month if we went up against these guys."

"So, what am I supposed to do – go home and wait for them to come knocking?"

Sheehan's head fell back against the chair. His eyes closed and he was silent for a moment. "Shit," he sighed bitterly. "You really fucked this up, Polito."

"Maybe, but I think it got fucked up when someone killed Bobby Coluccio and those two kids."

"You got that right." Sheehan sounded defeated.

Joe pressed his advantage. "There's one more thing I learned. Art doesn't have much time. He's got a date with a hit man tomorrow night."

"What are you talking about?"

"Art's going back to work. Somebody called the limo service and asked for him by name for Saturday night. If Art picks up that fare, I don't think we're ever going to see him again."

"What?" Sheehan sat up and stared at Joe. "That fucking idiot. He had plenty of money. He doesn't need to work."

"Maybe that wad of bills smelled like blood to him."

"What's that supposed to mean?"

"It means that money was supposed to keep him quiet about the Coluccio killings. In Art's frame of mind, it probably just made him feel more guilty."

Sheehan's mouth curled in an angry sneer. "Let's get one thing straight right now. I had nothing to do with those killings. That was an accident – wrong people, wrong place, wrong time. I didn't want Coluccio dead. And those kids – my god…"

"But Art was involved in the 'accident,' or he knew about it. Didn't he?"

"Yeah, alright," Sheehan nodded. "That's what's eating him. But it wasn't his fault, either. That's what's fucked up about all this."

"If it's so fucked up, why are you working so hard to keep it secret?"

"Mostly because I don't want to see Art end up dead."

"Good," Joe said forcefully. "Neither do I. What do we do?"

"We," Sheehan stressed, "don't do anything. You go home and forget about it, and I take care of Art. You get it? I'm not working against you, but I'm not working with you, either."

"That's your call, but I'm not going home and forget about it. This thing's about to break, and when it does, Art's going to need all the help he can get."

"You can't help him."

"That's what you keep telling me."

"Yeah, but you don't listen. Maybe you'll believe me when you're lying in a ditch with a bullet in your head."

"Maybe," Joe said, "but maybe not. Like you said, I'm stubborn."

CHAPTER 21

Just finished with his shift, Chad Reese was home, changing out of his uniform when his cell phone started playing the hip-hop tune he was using for a ring tone. He picked it up off the dresser. The number was vaguely familiar, but he couldn't immediately place it. He flipped it open.

"Yeah?" he said in a noncommittal tone.

"What?" he suddenly exploded at the phone, his face contorting into an expression of shock and anger. "You can't drop it like that. How am I going to get someone on him? How do I know where to pick him up? ... You can't do this. I'll go back to the organization. You won't work again...."

Chad listened for a moment and was about to respond when the phone went dead. He slapped it shut and stared at himself in the mirror. His eyes were dark with impotent fury and his jaw clenched so hard the muscles stood out in ridges at the side of his face.

A minute later, when his breathing had returned to normal, he picked up the phone and pulled up a number from the speed dial. It was answered on the second ring.

"It's me," Chad said. "We got a problem. That guy you got for the tail fucked up, claims he got spotted. He walked off the job.... Pro my ass. He was useless. We got to get somebody else."

Chad listened for a minute, his face showing more and more dismay. "Me?" he whined. "I can't. I'm on duty. I can't be babysitting Polito.... I know it's just tomorrow.... I know he could fuck it up, but ...."

His shoulders sagged. "Yeah, alright. I'll call in sick." He snapped the phone shut, and the eyes that stared back at him from the mirror were clouded with uncertainty and fear.

The visitor's flight was due in at 7:30, and the airline said it was on time. Traffic through the tunnel was jammed and Reese got to the terminal at 7:35. He had to fight his way into the pack of cars shuffling through the pickup lane, but finally managed to pull up to the curb, where he settled down to wait. Reese had no idea what the guy looked like, so there was no point looking for him. The visitor had the make, model and license of Chad's car. He'd find it. Reese leaned back in the seat and turned up the volume on the hip-hop station.

He hadn't been there more than a couple minutes, when he was startled by someone tapping at his driver-side window. It was a state trooper motioning him to move along. Reese hit the button that slid down the window.

"I'm just waiting to pick up a friend," he said, putting on a humble smile.

"You can't sit here," the statey said, not bothering to look at him. "Move it."

"Just a couple minutes, officer. His flight landed 10 minutes ago."

"No exceptions. Move it." The trooper was already waving his arms at the cars behind Reese.

Reese thought about pulling out his badge, looking for a little professional courtesy, but caught himself in time. He wasn't sure how much a Somerville shield would count for outside the jurisdiction, and he realized that it would probably mark him in the trooper's blond, crew-cut head. He couldn't afford that, so he gritted his teeth in frustration and complied, racing around the half-mile circumferential drive that connected the four terminals of the airport, getting back in the pack of waiting cars in less than 5 minutes.

This time, when he pulled to the curb, a man who had been standing on the broad sidewalk in front of the terminal detached himself from the milling crowd and strode toward Reese's car. The man was of average height, in his 40's, with a deep tan that looked out of place in the cold and dark of a winter evening in Boston. He wore leather gloves, a stylish black fedora, and a black wool overcoat over a dark gray suit. His white dress shirt was open at the neck, with no tie, and he carried a small overnight bag.

The man tried to open the car door, but the automatic locks had clicked in. Reese scrambled to hit the unlock button. The locks clicked open and the man opened the door.

"Sorry," Reese said. "The automatic locking thing – I forgot."

The man slid into the seat. "Reese?" he asked softly, staring straight ahead through the windshield.

"Uh, yeah. Trudell?"

The man smiled without looking at him, almost as if he was smiling to himself. "Right."

Reese had to wait for the trooper to wave the cars along before he could get out to the main drive and take the exit for the new Ted Williams tunnel. "I thought I'd show you the pick up spot for tomorrow night," Reese volunteered.

"Don't bother. I know the Parker House. You got the money?"

"Of course. There's an envelope in the glove compartment."

"Good." Trudell took the envelope out of the glove compartment and put it in his pocket.

"Aren't you going to count it?" Reese asked, a weak joke.

"Why?" Trudell's reply was icy. "Did you take a little out for yourself?"

"Huh? No, no. I was just ..." Reese realized his visitor was not in the mood for jokes. "It's all there," he said lamely.

"Good." The man let his head roll back against the headrest and closed his eyes.

Reese's face started to burn and the muscles in his jaw tensed. This guy was treating him like some goddamn immigrant cab driver. Did he understand that he, Reese, had planned and initiated this whole mission? Of course, contact had been made through the organization, but nothing would have happened without Reese calling for it. Maybe Trudell needed a little reminder who he was working for.

"The guy's picture's in the envelope, too," Reese said stiffly.

"Good." Trudell didn't open his eyes.

"I got some ideas where you could have him drive you," Reese said, with an edge of irritation surfacing in his voice, "so you'd have a nice quiet place to do it."

Trudell turned to him for the first time and fixed him with a cold and empty stare. His voice was like the rumble of distant thunder. "Listen. I don't want your fucking half-assed ideas. All I want from you is my money and a ride to the Four Seasons. Once I step out of this car, I don't want to see your face again, and you sure as hell don't want to see mine. Because, if you do, it means something went wrong, and my face will be the last one you ever see."

Reese's mouth hung open, and a shudder rippled down his spine. The stranger leaned back again and closed his eyes. Reese turned back to the road in a trance that was broken when he saw that the car was drifting into the next lane. He corrected with a jerk of the wheel and let out the breath he had been unconsciously holding. He drove on in silence, and the killer never opened his eyes until the car stopped in front of the hotel on Boylston Street. A doorman opened the car door and Trudell stepped out, carrying his overnight bag. He gave the doorman a bill, but did not glance back at Reese or say a word, disappearing quickly behind the smoked glass doors. The doorman shut the door and Reese pulled away from the curb, suddenly aware of the pressure in his chest that threatened to choke him.

CHAPTER 22

When he got home, Joe put a can of soup in a pan and set it on the gas. While it was heating, he called Eileen Merrill. He wouldn't admit it, even to himself, but he was anxious to hear her voice.

"Hello?" a man answered.

"Oh, uh, I was calling for Eileen Merrill."

"Yes. Who is this?"

"Joe Polito."

After a short pause, the man said, "I'll get her."

"Hello?" Eileen's voice was formal.

"Who was that?" Joe whispered, "your husband?"

"Yes, Joe. What have you got?"

"What do you mean?... Oh. He's still there. What do you want me to do, hang up?"

"No, no, that won't be necessary."

"Then what? You want to call me back when you're free?"

"No, that's alright," she said in the same cool tones, then shifted down to an urgent whisper. "I'll be at your place in an hour."

"But what about ..."

"That's fine. I'll talk with you then."

"But ..."

"Goodbye."

The line went dead. Joe clicked his phone shut and stared at it with an angry frown. "Shit," he said out loud.

About half an hour later, Joe was washing the soup pan when his phone started chirping at him. He dried his hands and picked it up. The number that was calling was not one he recognized.

"Hello?"

"Joe Polito?" Another unknown male voice.

"Yeah?"

"This is Officer Reese with Somerville PD. I'm working the Delaney missing persons case. I understand you're interested in it, too." Reese was working hard to maintain a professional tone, but he couldn't hide his distaste.

"That's right."

"You stopped by the station this morning. What'd you want?"

"I thought we could compare notes. Mrs. Merrill told me you were making some progress on her father's case. That's more than I can say."

Reese paused for a moment, weighing the situation. "I've done a basic investigation. I wouldn't say it's turned up much."

"She said you were looking into the possibility that one of Mr. Delaney's friends might have died, causing him to become depressed or guilt-stricken?" Joe left it hanging in the air, an open question.

Again, Reese took his time. "It's a routine question."

"So you didn't have anyone in mind?"

"No."

"But you knew when it happened." The question had become an accusation.

"I didn't know anything," Reese said, unable to suppress the anger in his voice. "Mrs. Merrill said her father had been depressed for a month or so. I wondered if the death of one of his friends might have caused it. That's all."

"What do you think now?" Joe did not react to Reese's tone.

"I don't think anything," Reese snarled, "and they don't pay me to answer your god damn questions."

"That's alright," Joe said evenly, "you can consider me Mrs. Merrill's representative. They do pay you to answer to her."

"I'll consider you nothing. She hasn't authorized you for anything."

"Then I'll have her speak to you. I'm sure the chief would like to know how little you've helped on this."

"The chief isn't going to listen to a fucking thing you've got to say. Your name is shit around here."

"Funny, I've heard the same about you."

"That's bullshit. They wouldn't dare badmouth me. I've got enough juice to bounce them out of here."

"Don't count on it, asshole. Your juice is drying up."

"Fuck you, Polito. And stay out of my way or I'll pound you into the pavement."

"I hope you try."

Polito hung up on Reese's hysterical cursing. He wore a satisfied grin as he went back to straightening up.

Eileen showed up about 9:00. She rang the bell, and Joe buzzed her in. When he opened the door to his apartment, she stood there with a brown paper bag in one hand and a crooked smile on her lips.

"I brought you a present," she said, handing him the bag, which held a bottle.

Joe pulled her inside and kissed her. He closed the door and pulled the bottle out of the bag. It was a fifth of Blanton's Bourbon.

"Well," he smiled, "the good stuff. Thanks."

He knew the Blanton's was well out of his price range and only pocket change to her. He thought he should resent it, but he didn't. There was something appealing in her apprehensive smile.

"Let's open it," she said.

He hung up her coat, and she followed him into the kitchen, where he put ice cubes into short glasses and poured the expensive liquor over them. He gave her one of the glasses and raised the other.

"To Art," he said.

"Right," she sighed, distractedly. "To Art."

Joe sipped his drink and watched her, suddenly aware that she was strung as tight as a piano. "What's wrong," he asked.

"It's Mark. He's all ... I don't know. He got angry after you called. I think he has some suspicion you're not just helping me find my father. It was awful."

"I thought you said you'd be glad if he showed some interest."

She uttered a short, bitter laugh. "Not this kind. He doesn't give a shit what I do unless it bruises his tender ego. I guess picking up a call from my lover was too much for him. Now he's talking about divorce."

"Is that bad? To be honest, you don't seem like you care much about him."

"I don't know what I want from him. I'm worried what a divorce would do to Jake. God knows he's put up with enough from the two of us already."

"Jake must know how things are between you. Maybe a divorce would clear the air – you know, bring it out in the open where you can all deal with it."

"Maybe," she said doubtfully. "Maybe I'm just afraid to deal with it."

"I didn't think you were afraid of anything."

"That's my public face." Her voice trembled. "This is the real one - afraid of everything."

"That's not true," Joe said soothingly.

He led her into the front room and they sat on the sofa. Eileen swallowed half her drink and let her head fall back on the cushions. "You must think we're pretty strange, living together in that big house with nothing in common but a kid and a few bank accounts."

"We're all strange, if you look deep enough."

"Yes, but some people are strangely happy, and that's not happening in our house. That's why it's so important that we find Art. He's the only bright spot in Jake's life."

"Why shouldn't you be happy, too?"

"I don't even think about that," she said bitterly. "I wouldn't know how."

"You might surprise yourself."

She shook her head. "Not unless I can make Jake happy first."

"You mean I'm not enough?" Joe's tone was light, joking, but the question was real.

She put her arms around his neck and drew him close, staring into his eyes with deadly seriousness. "You're more than enough, Joe. It's me who's not enough. I've been living a lie so long, I don't know what to do with someone like you."

"I guess that makes us even," Joe said. "I don't know what to do with someone like you."

"Just keep doing what you're doing," she sighed and kissed him.

Later, when the heat between them had cooled to a gentle warmth, they lay in bed looking up at the two rectangles of light on the wall, and Joe gave her a quick progress report. He told her about Pat Sheehan picking up Art from Sunday mass and taking him off into hiding, about the limo service and Art's intention to continue working. He said Art was trying to get right with some things that happened in the distant past, back when he and Sheehan were involved with the Somerville rackets. He didn't tell her what he knew about Betty Coluccio and Art's apparent guilt over the slaughter of her family, nor did he mention the threat of Art's Saturday evening appointment and the ominous attention of the little man with the big nose. There was no need to horrify her or frighten her with the implied threat to her father, especially when she was already overwhelmed by the strain of her own domestic situation.

Eileen listened without comment. When Joe was done, she simply asked, "What do we do, now?"

"I'm going to talk to Art tomorrow, and I think Pat Sheehan will, too. After that, we should know where we stand." Joe could hear how lame this sounded, and he rushed on to try to reassure her. "I don't think your father is in any danger of … hurting himself, but I don't quite understand why he's in hiding, or what it'll take to get him back. I think I'm going to ask him to call you. Maybe it would help for him to talk about it with you and Jake."

"Maybe," she said, but her voice seemed small and hopeless.

Joe could think of nothing to say to lift her out of this morbid state. They lay silent, side by side in Joe's bed, their minds wandering on separate paths.

With nothing to direct his thoughts, Joe found himself replaying the call from Chad Reese in his head. He was aware of the unfounded anger he felt toward the officer. Was it just the residue of bitterness from his own history with Somerville PD? Was it second-hand resentment he'd somehow picked up from Paul Shea and Eileen? He had never met the man. How could he hate him? But he did. He felt an impatient desire to confront the arrogant son-of-a-bitch and smash his face into the pavement. It wasn't fair, and it wasn't right, but there it was, a nervous twitch in his shoulders that would not be satisfied but by blood.

Eileen rolled toward him and gently rested her arm on his chest, pulling him back from his brutal reverie. The streetlight was cool and pale in the room, filling it with shadows. "Joe?" she said softly, to see if he was awake.

"Yeah?"

"What did you mean when you said you didn't know what to do with me?"

"What did you mean when you said it about me?" Joe answered lightly.

"I don't know," she said in a soft wistful voice. "I guess I've been trying to fit you into my life, and I don't know how. You're not like the people I know. You don't worry about what people think of you. If you decide to do something, you do it. So much of what I do is for show. I don't know how to be like you, and I'm so afraid you'll see through me and not like what you see."

Joe laughed softly. "That's funny. It's only when I see through you that I do like what I see. My problem is there's so much to see through – the house, the car, the job, the clothes, the money. It's like you're from another planet. It's only when we get past all that stuff that I see we're not that far apart. But that's not easy for me, either."

She snuggled close, and Joe was surprised when he felt tears pool on his chest. "I don't know what to do, Joe. It feels like my life is coming apart."

"Because of me?"

"No," she moaned. "You're the best thing I've got. It's just that when I'm with you, I see all the rest of it so clearly, it hurts."

"Maybe you shouldn't be with me."

"Don't say that. If I didn't have you, I'd be totally lost."

"What about after we find Art, and you don't have any more reason to see me? What happens then?"

"I don't know. Would you still want to see me?"

"Of course, but I don't think you're husband is going to get any happier about it."

"No. That's true, and it's a problem."

"Yeah," Joe said doubtfully, "I guess it is."

"Why do you say it like that? Don't you believe me?"

"I believe you. But I still don't get it. If he means as little to you as you say, why don't you leave him?"

"It's not that easy. I've got to think of Jake."

"Okay, but I can't think your family life is any better for him than it is for you."

"That's where you're wrong. Mark and I do everything we can to make it good for him. Most of his friends' parents are divorced or separated or bitter. Somehow, we've managed to convince Jake that we're different. I think we both use work to hide the fact that we aren't really a couple anymore. It puts a lot of stress on us, but so far, I think it's worked."

"But don't you see how screwed up that is? Don't you want to change it?"

"Yes, but I'm terrified I'll just make it worse."

Joe shook his head and scowled into the dark. "I don't know," he muttered, trying to imagine what could be worse.

CHAPTER 23

Saturday morning was bleak. Joe got up around 7:00, made himself a cup of coffee and sat by the window watching the snow fall. The temperature was stuck just above freezing, melting the wet flakes as they hit the pavement in front of the house.

Eileen had left his bed about midnight. Joe didn't ask what kind of a story she planned to tell her husband. What happened between them was none of his business, and he was happy to leave it that way. These nights with Eileen were a sudden and unexpected gift of fate, but they could end just as quickly and inexplicably. Joe had been through enough women in his 40 years to know that the outcome was mostly out of his hands. He could only let it happen, and that was fine with him, since he wasn't sure what he wanted from it anyway.

He picked up his book and managed to clear his head enough to make it through another 20 pages, struggling to keep the names matched with the characters and situations. Joe enjoyed the challenge of trying to imaginatively inhabit a culture and psychology so foreign, but his own situation continued to pluck at his sleeve, reminding him there were endings to be worked out in the real world, as well.

At 8:00, his phone rang. He answered it eagerly, with a sense of relief. "Hello?"

"Joe, it's Paul. Hope I didn't wake you."

"No, no. I've been up for an hour. What's up?"

"Well, maybe nothing," Paul said uncertainly, "but it's just a weird little coincidence I thought you should know about."

"What?"

"You know how I said this Somerville cop, Chad Reese, was taking an unusual interest in the Delaney case and talking about you and Tommy?"

"Right."

"I ran into him this morning. I mean, I saw him. I was coming into the coffee shop down in Davis just as he ducked out the other door. I think he saw me and didn't want me to see him – which makes sense. I can't stand the guy and he probably knows it. But then I started wondering what he was doing over here in Davis. His territory is East Somerville and he lives in Charlestown. So what's he doing over here at 7:00 on a Saturday morning? Then I remembered he's supposed to be on duty. Why is he in street clothes? It bothered me enough to call the station. Christine, the new dispatcher told me he called in sick. I don't know what any of that means, but I thought it might have something to do with Art Delaney and you, so I thought you should know."

"Jesus," Joe breathed. "Thanks, Paul. That's good to know."

"You wouldn't want to tell me what this is about, would you?"

"Believe me, I'd tell you if I knew something. Right now, it's just a bunch of questions. Where's Art? What's he doing? Why is this Chad Reese so interested? I don't have any answers yet, but I think I'm getting close."

"Alright," Shea said skeptically, "but let me know when you get something, especially if it's police business."

"I will. But there's one other thing you could help me with."

"What's that?"

"What does this Reese look like? I don't think I've ever seen him."

"That's easy enough. About 6 feet, 180, dark hair, mustache, regular features, kind of handsome, around 30."

"What was he wearing?"

"Only thing I noticed was a leather coat, dark leather, looked expensive."

"That's great, Paul. Thanks again. Thanks for thinking of me."

"No problem."

Joe walked up to the sandwich shop for breakfast, just as he had the day before and many days before that, but this time it was for something more than food. He had his eggs and toast, drank another cup of coffee and read the Globe, but the routine was cover for his real purpose, which was to spot his tail – whether it was the little hook-nosed man or Chad Reese. While he read the paper, he would occasionally glance out the window to the park across the street.

Once, when he looked up, he got a glimpse of someone in a dark coat. The man was walking along the ridge that runs through the little park, just about to disappear behind the crest of the hill, quite a distance – maybe sixty to seventy yards - from where Joe sat in the sandwich shop. He was hatless, with dark hair, but he was faced somewhat away from Joe and the light was behind him. Joe thought he might have had a mustache. There was no way to be sure it was Chad Reese, but Joe thought it best to assume that he was still being followed.

He had to fight the urge to run up over the hill, find the man in the dark coat, and stomp his face. It wasn't time for that yet. All his life Joe had battled the impulsiveness that rose up inside him and demanded action without regard to timing or consequences. Often, the consequences had not been favorable. This time, he promised himself, would be different. He went home and waited.

At 11:00, his cell phone rang. He flipped it open. "Hello?"

"Joe, it's Eileen." A shudder rippled through her voice. "Art called Jake again. I'm afraid he's going to do something. Jake was upset and crying. He thinks his grandfather is going to die."

"Wait, wait," Joe said, trying to slow it down, trying to understand. "Did you talk to him?"

"No. I'm at work. Anna called and told me. Jake took the call and after he hung up, he just went to pieces. I'm not sure what Art told him, but Jake got the idea he was saying goodbye, that he'd never see him again. Joe, I don't know what to do. We've got to do something."

"Okay, yeah. But what did he say?"

"Oh, I don't know. Anna doesn't know what's going on, and Jake probably wasn't making much sense. It just sounded like more of that horrible guilt." Eileen paused for a moment, as if pulling herself back from the edge of panic. Then she said, as if she was just hearing it again, "No, no wait … he said he wanted Jake to know he didn't do anything bad. It's just that he knew about something bad and he kept it secret for so long it made him sick inside and guilty just like the people that did it. But he wanted Jake to know he loved him and he hoped he could forgive him."

"Did he say anything about what he was going to do?"

"No, but Anna saw where he was calling from. It was the St. Michael's Retreat Center in Dorchester. Can you go there and try to get him? Try to keep him from harming himself?"

"Of course I can, but aren't you coming?"

"I'm all the way out in Westborough and I'm in this huge meeting," she said in a rush. "It'd take me more than an hour to get there, and I don't know what I could say to him. I'm afraid I'd make it worse. We're not that close. I think you'd be better to reason with him."

Joe was silent for a moment, frowning thoughtfully at the phone. "Alright. I'll go, but stick close to your phone, okay? And I might want to call Jake, too."

"Okay, Joe. But try not to scare him anymore than he already is. This thing could leave a scar."

"I'll be careful, but I'll bet Jake would want to talk to him. He might be stronger than you think."

"Maybe," she said bleakly.

"One other thing," Joe said. "I need you to authorize me to spend some money, more than you gave me. I've got an idea how we might get Art off the hook, but it could be pretty expensive."

"Joe, you know that won't be a problem."

"I didn't think so." Joe's voice held a slight edge of bitterness. "I may be able to swing this without cash, but you might get a call to make a credit card payment."

"That's fine. Call me when you know something."

"I will."

Joe shuffled mechanically to the window. The snow had stopped, but patches of white frosted the tiny bits of lawn and garden in front of the houses across the street. Joe didn't see it. He was picturing a young boy alone in a big empty house, confused and crying by a telephone. Joe picked up the phone and dialed Pat Sheehan.

"Hello?" he heard Rose answer.

"Hi, Rose. This is Joe Polito. Is Pat available?"

"Oh, Joe, I'm so glad you called. Pat left almost an hour ago and he wouldn't say where he was going. He's so weak, I didn't want him to go, but he wouldn't listen. Do you have any idea where he might have gone?"

"Yeah," Joe sighed, "but it probably won't do us any good. He's too damn stubborn to let us help him."

"But where?" Rose asked helplessly.

"He probably went after Art, probably at St. Michael's Retreat in Dorchester. Does Pat know anybody there?"

"St. Michael's? Yes, yes. I think he does. An old friend of his is a priest there, Father Andrews."

"Can you call him and find out if Pat or Art are there, see if you can convince them to come back?"

"I'll try."

"Okay. Call me back after you talk to them, whatever you get."

"I will, Joe. I'll call you right back.

Joe sat by the window and looked out at the street with a blank expression that stayed that way until the phone rang two minutes later. Rose was on the line, breathless.

"Joe, Pat was there, but he picked up Art and they left. I talked to Father Andrews and he was nice, but he didn't know where they went."

"Does Pat have a cell phone," Joe asked. "I mean, have you tried to call him?"

"He doesn't have one. He doesn't like them."

"Me either. Can you think of anywhere Pat might go with Art? Pat must be exhausted. They're not going to ride around all day."

"I hope they'd come here."

"I know, but any other place?"

"Not really. I guess they might go to a bar or something, but Pat doesn't really have a favorite place like that. He doesn't go out much anymore."

"Then there's no sense to go look for them. They could be anywhere. I'm going to try something to keep Art from getting killed. If you talk to Pat, get him to call me, and if he won't, you call me and tell me what he told you, even if it seems like nothing. Just keep in touch. I'll call you if I hear from them. Okay?"

"Okay. And thanks, Joe. You make me feel like we're doing something."

"It's not much," Joe muttered, "but I guess it's better than nothing."

CHAPTER 24

Joe put on a fleece-lined cloth jacket and walked down to the square. The sky had partly cleared, and broken clouds were being hustled along on a cold wind. At the Red Line station, he took the stairs down to the subway platform. He did not see any sign of a tail, probably because he was careful not to look for one.

The platform was between the two tracks. Inbound trains loaded on one side, outbound on the other. It was midday on a Saturday. There were a couple dozen people on the platform, most waiting for the inbound train. On a seat facing the stairs, a man played a recorder with accompaniment from some kind of battery powered device. The piece sounded classical or even medieval, lending a sedate and orderly context to the random sounds of conversation that hummed and muttered in the tunnel. Joe stood in front of the musician and watched him play.

An electronic voice rose above the other sounds and said, "The train to Alewife is approaching the station." A few seconds later, the rumble and screech could be heard, rapidly growing in volume until the train slowed and stopped on the outbound side. The doors slid open and people got off. Joe waited for them and then got on.

Chad Reese had been standing near the end of the platform, hidden from Joe by the stairs, but keeping track of him. He was surprised that Joe got on the outbound train, but he waited until the doors were about to close, then jumped onto the car two ahead of Joe's.

Alewife station is the end of the line, just one stop outbound from Davis. As a major hub of public transit, the station includes a bus terminal, a few small retail businesses – fast food, flowers, newsstand – and a four story parking garage, all clustered around a large open hall. When he got off the train, Joe went up the stairs and crossed to the escalator that took him up to the third floor of the parking garage. From there, he entered an enclosed stairwell to get to the top floor. On weekdays the garage inevitably filled with commuters' cars by 8 AM, but on Saturdays, it filled slowly from the bottom up, and the top floor often stayed nearly empty all day.

The escalator is open to the main hall, where Chad stood, off to the side, watching Joe ascend. When Joe went into the stairwell, Chad sprinted across the hall and bolted up the escalator. He went into the stairwell and raced up the steps. The door into the garage had a small glass panel criss-crossed with a reinforcing wire mesh. Chad paused and looked through the glass. There were only a few parked cars scattered around on the wide expanse of blacktop, and there was no one in sight. He cautiously opened the door and poked his head through.

Joe grabbed the collar of Chad's leather coat and pulled the rest of him through the door, which swung shut behind him. It caught Chad off guard, and his resistance was weak and ineffectual. Joe was four inches shorter, but just as heavy, and much more powerful than Chad. He also had much more experience at street fighting. Chad struggled to get to the gun in his shoulder holster, but the stiff leather coat and Joe's insistent aggression prevented it. After a brief scuffle, Joe had him pinned against a concrete wall with his left arm bent painfully behind him. Joe knew how to apply just enough pressure on Chad's twisted arm to keep him still.

"What do you want?" Chad grunted between teeth clenched in pain and fury.

Joe had seen Chad's effort to reach into his coat. "First, I want that gun" he said, reaching around to rip open the expensive leather coat, popping off two of the buttons in the process. He eased the gun out of the holster and glanced at it. It was a stubby .38 caliber revolver, not the standard issue of the Somerville PD. Joe shoved it into his jacket pocket.

"Now, who are you?" he asked.

"None of your fucking business." Chad had recovered enough to bluster.

"I think it is," Joe said evenly. "I think you were following me, and I don't like that. So tell me your name." Joe pushed the twisted arm up another half inch.

Chad yelped involuntarily. "David Williams," he gasped, picking a name at random.

"Is it?" Joe said. "Let's see." With his free hand, he lifted the tails of the coat and pulled a wallet from Chad's back pocket. He flipped open the wallet and Chad's driver's license was displayed in a plastic sleeve.

"You lied to me, Chad."

"Fuck you," Chad said, but he was still in pain and there was little conviction behind it.

"Now I want to know why you're following me. Who are you trying to protect?" Joe eased up slightly on the arm.

"I'm not following you, and you're in deep shit."

"No," Joe said. "You are following me. And I'm not going to have any trouble from you."

Chad suddenly used his free arm to push away from the wall. At the same time, he leaped awkwardly in the air to try to free his twisted left arm. Joe took a step back with Chad's lunge and pushed the arm past its limit. Something popped in Chad's shoulder as he came down and he gasped. Joe released his arm and took another step back, leaving the next move to Chad.

Chad turned to face him. He was bent forward slightly at the waist. His left arm hung limp at his side, and he held his injured shoulder with his right hand. There was an animal look of fear and hatred in his eyes. "You son-of-a-bitch," he groaned. "I'll kill you."

"No you won't," Joe said. "But I still want to know why you're following me, who you're working for."

"Fuck you," Chad breathed as he lunged at Joe, trying to hit him with a looping right hand.

Joe avoided it easily, stepping inside and dropping Chad to the blacktop with a solid knee to the groin. Chad let out a high pitched yelp and collapsed to the pavement. He curled into a fetal position with a rhythmic rocking motion, his breath coming in short hiccupping gasps. Joe stood over him looking down coldly.

"I'd love to stay here and keep trying to get you to tell me what you're up to, Chad, but I've got other things to do," he said. He took a piece of nylon cord from the pocket of his jeans and wrestled Chad's left hand behind his back. Chad put up little resistance. Joe tied the cord tightly around Chad's wrist, then pulled his right hand next to it and wrapped the cord twice around the two wrists. He looped the cord between Chad's arms and wound it around the binding, pulling it tight and knotting it. He quickly did the same to Chad's ankles.

Chad was still in the fetal position, rocking and moaning, effectively immobilized. The entire process had taken less than 5 minutes, but Joe had been lucky. In that time, no one had come up to the fourth floor to park or retrieve their car. Joe picked up Chad's wallet and tossed it over the railing. He was walking through the swinging door back to the stairs when he heard the faint slap of the wallet hitting the pavement below.

He caught the first inbound train and got off at Kendall. He made a fancy little loop around the Cambridge Police Station to spot any new tail he might have developed, but he didn't see any. By the time he went into Luxury Limo, he was fairly certain that no one was following him.

Al Trautman was sitting at the desk behind the counter, exactly where he'd been the day before. When Joe came in, he looked up and smiled. "Well," he said, "I was worried you wouldn't show, but here you are."

"Yup," Joe grinned, reaching into his wallet and extracting a thick wad of hundred dollar bills. "Here I am, and have I got a deal for you."

"Wonderful." Trautman's eyes wandered to the stack of bills that Joe put on the counter.

"First, you hear anything more from Art – or about him?"

"Not since I talked to you last night."

"I think I still owe you for that one." Joe took the top bill from the stack and slid it across the counter.

Trautman stood up and stepped to the counter. He picked up the bill, folded it twice and put it into a small zippered pocket in his quilted vest. He zipped up the pocket and smiled at Joe. "You mentioned a deal," he prompted.

"Yes," Joe said, leaning over the counter conspiratorially. "I want to drive for you tonight. I want to take Art's appointment."

"Hm." Trautman paused. He seemed perplexed. "I couldn't get the paperwork done – background checks and such – I couldn't get all that done in time to make it legal."

"I know, but what's supposed to happen in that car tonight isn't legal anyway, and if I drive, I don't think you'll have any complaints coming back at you."

Trautman looked into Joe's face with a frankly appraising expression. "I'm inclined to trust you, Joe. You've been straight with me so far. Can you tell me any more?"

"I can tell you what you need to know," Joe said seriously, "but there's some of it you'll just have to trust me on – and that's for your own protection. But the first thing you need to know is that stack of bills is all yours if you help me. On top of any expenses or damages, you keep it, clear and tax-free. How does that sound?"

"Very interesting," Al Trautman said, fanning the bills for a quick count. "Tell me what I have to do."

Joe spent half an hour with Trautman explaining what he needed. Al made a few calls and lined things up. It wasn't easy, but it looked like it might work. When Joe left Luxury Limo to grab the subway downtown, he met Al's mechanic coming in. The guy was a heavy set young kid in a black leather motorcycle jacket. He had long stringy hair and a full beard. His hand had a permanent patina of black grease.

Joe shook it anyway. "Don't let me down," he said with mock seriousness. "I'm counting on you."

"Don't worry man," the kid grinned. One of his front teeth was silver. "Al told me what you need. I got you covered."

Joe took the subway to Downtown Crossing and went into one of the department stores, where he spent a couple hours getting fitted to a black suit, black tie, and black shoes, with a white shirt to go with them. A black, short-brimmed cap to complete his chauffeur's outfit was harder. He had to visit several different stores before he found one that looked the part. It was 5:00 before he was done.

He still had a couple hours to kill, and he was getting hungry. He walked over to that strange little triangle of no-man's land wedged between Government Center and the North End, between the new Boston Garden and the old Haymarket, an unreclaimed collection of buildings that were neither new nor historic, in a city that was becoming nothing but one or the other. Joe liked the dingy feel of the old city that lingered in those doomed streets, even as new businesses took over space in the tired buildings.

One of the new businesses was a brew pub that served their own beer, made on the premises. The beer was fantastic and the food was decent, but the place was packed. The Bruins were playing at 7:00, and the pre-game crowd was having a good beer and a good meal before they subjected themselves to the over-priced, watered down beer and tasteless, reheated food of the Garden. Joe talked to the young girl at the door and found it would be a twenty minute wait even for a single at the bar. He put his name in and went back out to the street.

He walked half a block and found a doorway that was somewhat protected from the noise of the street.

He looked up the call from Rose and let his phone dial her number.

"Hello." Rose's voice was urgent. "Joe, did he call you?"

"No. Why, did you talk to him?"

"Yes, he finally called half an hour ago. I begged him to call you. The only reason I didn't call was I didn't want your line to be busy."

"That's alright. What did he say?"

"He wouldn't tell me where he was, but he said Art was with him, and they would be alright. He sounded so tired and weak. I don't know if he's strong enough to take all this."

"He seems pretty determined. Maybe stubborn is the better word. He won't let me help him."

"His pride won't let him, but it's so hard to see him burn himself up like this when he's got so little time left."

Joe was silent for a moment. "Did he say when he'd be home?"

"No, but he said he had a place for them to stay. They wouldn't have to spend the night on the street."

"Good. That's the important thing. Maybe by tomorrow some of this will be cleared up."

"I hope so. I'm very worried about them – both of them."

"They'll be alright," Joe said, wincing at the comforting lie.

Joe called Eileen and told her her father was with Sheehan, safe for the night. She was at home in Lexington with Jake and Anna. Mark was on his way to Logan, flying overnight to London. She was relieved that Art was not in immediate danger, but she sounded distracted.

"Jake's a mess. He says he doesn't want any dinner, even though Anna's making him his favorite, macaroni and cheese. Now, I'm just hoping he'll go to bed at a reasonable hour. Joe, could you come out here tonight? I don't want to be alone."

"I don't know about tonight. I got a couple things I got to do first."

"Well, maybe I could come in to your place."

"Yeah, maybe. Let's see how it goes. I'll call you when I'm done."

Joe went back to the restaurant, ate his dinner and had a cup of coffee to keep his wits sharp. It wasn't quite seven when he left the brew pub. He could have taken the T to Kendall but decided to walk instead. It was less than two miles. He had the time, and the cool air and the walk would give him a chance to clear his head.

In twenty minutes, he was on the Longfellow Bridge, crossing the Charles River, and thinking he should have taken the T. The cool air turned into a cold wind sweeping down the river, biting through his jacket, stinging his nose and ears. A thin crust of ice was forming in patches on the river. The suit pants weren't meant for warmth, and he carried the suit coat in a bag, since it wouldn't fit under his jacket. The chauffeur's cap helped, but he had to hold the brim down to keep the wind from carrying it out onto the river. Joe was the only pedestrian on the bridge.

His phone rang, and he dug it out of his pocket. The number wasn't one he knew, but he flipped it open.

"Hello," he yelled above the wind.

"For Chrissakes, I can hear you, Joe. I'm not deaf."

"What?" Joe yelled louder, turning away from the wind to try to hear the voice on the phone.

"I said I can hear you. Stop shouting."

"Oh. Who's this?"

"It's me, Pat Sheehan. Where are you, anyway? It sounds like you're in a fucking wind tunnel."

"I'm in the middle of the Longfellow Bridge, freezing my balls off."

"What the fuck are you doing there?"

"I'm going over to Kendall to take Art's job."

"What? I spent the whole goddamn day talking Art out of it. Now you want to take it?"

"You got a better idea? You keep telling me these guys are serious. I believe you. They're not going to stop because you've got Art out of the way for a few days."

"So what are you going to do to stop them?"

"I want to send them a message that Art's not the problem. There's other people that know what happened. They knock off Art, those other people aren't going to keep quiet."

"Yeah? Well what's to keep them from going after those other people, starting with you, tonight, right there in the cab? If this guy's really a pro, he's going to whack you just for being there."

"I'm not going to let him."

"Christ," Sheehan snorted in disgust. "You're going to get yourself killed for nothing. That bluff wouldn't fool a kid."

"Like I said, you got a better idea?"

The phone was silent for a long moment. Joe huddled with his back to the wind, facing a Boston skyline that glittered sharply against the black sky and broke into vague impressionistic patterns on the wind-ruffled, icy surface of the Charles.

"You're busting my balls, aren't you?" Sheehan finally said, with weary resignation. "This whole thing is just to get me to tell you what happened. Right?"

"No, but it would help."

Sheehan sighed. "Maybe. Maybe it'll just make it worse. At this point, I guess we got to roll the dice."

"That's what I'm saying."

"Alright. When you try to sell this bluff, there's one more thing you got to add to make it serious – the name of the guy who killed those kids."

"That would help."

"Or get you killed. It was Ed Reese."

CHAPTER 25

Joe forgot about the cold as he stood there on the bridge, listening to Pat Sheehan tell the story of how Bobby Coluccio and his kids were murdered. Sheehan's voice was hoarse and weary, but there was an unmistakable note of relief in it, as if in telling it, a small part of the weight was being lifted from his heart. Joe didn't ask any questions. He huddled to keep the phone out of the wind, hoping it wouldn't run out of juice and thinking of how he'd use what he was learning.

When he was through, Sheehan said, "I got to go make sure Art isn't wandering off. We're going to watch the Bruins, if I can make it through three periods."

"What do you mean?"

"I mean I'm fucking exhausted," Sheehan growled. "I'm not in shape for this kind of shit anymore."

He paused, then asked in a softer tone, "You still planning to get yourself killed tonight?"

"No. But I think what you gave me ups the odds I can make it work."

"I don't know why you want to run around after a bunch of fucked up old men. It's not your beef."

Joe thought of the look in Chad Reese's eyes as he lay on the pavement, trussed and groaning. "At this point, I think I made it mine," he said.

When he hung up from Pat Sheehan, Joe checked the battery on his phone. It was down to a single bar. He called Paul Shea and quickly relayed the story he'd just heard, leaving out only Art's name. He knew that Shea could easily guess who he was talking about, but there was no reason to make it

156

explicit. Before Shea could ask any questions, the phone died.

The calls used up his time cushion, and Joe had to hurry to Luxury Limo. When he got there, the young mechanic with the gray, grease-tinged hands had just completed the modifications to the limo. He was proud of his work and eager to demonstrate it to Joe. First it was the shield of bullet-proof glass that separated the front seat from the back.

The kid ran his hand over it fondly. "It'd take a cannon to break through that shit, man. I looked up the specs."

"Great," Joe grinned. "What about the seats? Could he shoot through there?"

"Not unless he wants to get killed by the ricochet. See that cloth panel. That's all new, covering a quarter inch of steel. No bullet's getting through that."

"Perfect. The locks?"

"Easy. I just put in a child-proofing kit. Probably should have had one anyway."

"How about the intercom."

"It's good," the kid said, with a slightly embarrassed shrug, "but there's still some feedback, since the back seat mic has to stay on. You got the volume control right there, and you might have to fiddle with it sometimes to cut the feedback. Sorry. If I had another hour and the right filters, I could fix it, but ..."

"That's okay. Now, what did I miss?"

The kid smiled. "The windows. I disabled the controls in the back seat, but there was no way to bullet-proof them. If the guy's smart enough and determined, he could break them out or shoot them out and reach around and shoot at you through your side window, or he could squeeze out through one of them."

"No problem. All I need is two minutes to give him the message. It's going to take that long for him to figure out what's going on. After that, he can do whatever he wants – except shoot me."

"This ought to give you the time, but it's a risk," the kid said, looking curiously into Joe's face. "You must have a pretty good reason to want to give this guy your message."

"Yeah," Joe said, looking away with sour discomfort, "I must."

As a licensed limo picking up a fare, Joe got a special reserved spot at the curb in front of the Parker House. He was ten minutes early – exactly as he had planned - and there didn't seem to be anyone waiting for him, though Joe wouldn't have known Trudell if he had been there. Joe parked and put the neatly printed plastic sign in the side window: "Luxury Limo, Mr. Trudell." He got back into the driver's seat and let his head fall forward as if he was asleep, his chauffeur's cap hiding his face. It was difficult to maintain that relaxed posture, difficult to resist the urge to lift up his head and look around for his fare, but Joe managed it for 10 minutes. It was a relief when he finally heard knuckles rapping at the passenger window.

He lifted his head and blinked, looking around as if it was taking him a moment to remember where he was. A man of about his own age was standing by the passenger door. He wore a charcoal wool topcoat, black leather gloves and a black broad-brimmed hat. The hat threw a shadow across his eyes, but Joe could see the look of impatient disdain that curled his lips.

Joe jumped out the driver's door and hustled around the limo to where the man waited on the sidewalk. "Sorry, sir," he was saying. "I must have dozed off. Been a long shift. Started airport runs at five this morning. Mr. Trudell?" He opened the rear door for the man to get into the limo.

Mr. Trudell looked confused. "But I was supposed to ... Art Delaney was supposed to drive for me."

"I know, sir," Joe said. "Art got held up in traffic coming back from his last run. The dispatcher asked me to come pick you up. We'll head right back to the yard and Art can take over from there. I got to get home and get some sleep."

Mr. Trudell frowned, but hesitantly slid into the back seat of the limo.

Joe pushed the door firmly shut and breathed a sigh of relief. The most critical step of the mission had been successfully completed. He hurried around the car and got into the driver's seat. As he pulled away from the curb, he glanced in the rear view mirror to see Mr. Trudell examining the back seat of the limo with an angry frown and growing mistrust.

"Wait," he said as Joe was turning onto Washington Street. The voice through the intercom was tinny, with a thin whining aura about it, the feedback Al Trautman's mechanic had mentioned. "I don't ... This is going to make me late."

"Don't worry. The yard is right across the river. Won't take 10 minutes. Where are you going?"

"I got to be in Lynn at 9:30," Trudell muttered.

"No sweat."

Trudell continued to examine the glass partition as the limo cruised down Cambridge Street. "What's this for?" Trudell asked, tapping the partition.

"Privacy." Joe grinned into the mirror. "You pull a curtain across and turn off the intercom, the back seat's as private as a bedroom. Some of our clients want to use it for that. For safety reasons, we only use the curtain when it's requested."

"Oh." Trudell thought about it. "But the glass is just regular glass, right?"

"What do you mean?"

"I mean, it's not special safety glass or bullet-proof, or anything like that?"

Joe frowned thoughtfully. "Jeez, I don't know. I doubt it."

Trudell sat back in the seat, but continued to look uneasy. He didn't unbutton his coat, and he left his hat and gloves on. Joe noted it, but waited until they were on the Longfellow Bridge, cruising past the spot where Joe got the call from Pat Sheehan, before he brought it up.

"Is it cold back there? I see you still got your gloves on."

"No, no." Trudell shook his head, managing a weak smile. "It's fine. I'm just not used to this weather."

"Haven't spent much time in Boston?"

"A couple times on business."

"How'd you happen to know Art?"

"He drove for me once before," Trudell said casually. "I remembered him."

"Huh." Joe seemed mildly surprised. "You followed him from that other outfit where he used to work?"

"Uh, yeah," Trudell mumbled. "Yeah, I did. They told me where he went."

Joe looked in the mirror with puzzled frown. "That's weird. They fired him because of his prison record. Why would they recommend him someplace else?"

"Don't know," Trudell muttered, turning away from Joe's inquiring gaze, to look out at the buildings of Kendall Square.

They were stopped at a light. Joe let it rest for a moment. When the light changed, he turned right on 3rd Street and said, "Seems kind of strange to me, how you're so interested in Art Delaney. What's the deal?"

Trudell turned toward the mirror, his eyes narrowed to angry slits, his jaw set like concrete. "I don't give a shit how it seems to you. You're a nosy son-of-a-bitch, and I'm done with you. Let me out here."

"I don't think so," Joe said. "There's something wrong with you. The Cambridge police station is right up here. Let's go talk to them and sort it out."

"What the fuck?" Trudell exploded, banging his fist against the glass. "Stop the car. I'm getting out."

"No," Joe said evenly, "you're not."

Joe had to stop to make the left onto Binney Street. Trudell yanked at the door handle and nothing happened. The door wouldn't open. He looked in the mirror, and Joe could see the panic growing behind the blind fury in his eyes. Joe made the turn.

"What is this?" Trudell yelled, his voice distorted into an electric screech by the feedback. "Let me out."

Joe did not respond. He drove down Binney, watching Trudell in the mirror.

Trudell's eyes darted around, trying to make sense of a senseless situation. He pushed and pulled at the window button. Nothing happened. He reached into his coat, but hesitated.

"We're almost there," Joe said, as he turned onto Fulkerson.

Trudell pulled a small automatic from inside his coat. Joe could see immediately that it was small caliber, .22 or possibly .25. If the glass was as good as the kid said, that little gun would hardly leave a scratch.

"Stop right here," Trudell snarled. He held the gun up, where he knew Joe could see it.

Joe glanced back, but continued driving.

"Stop or I'll blow your fucking brains out."

Joe turned onto Bent Street. He was pleased to see more than a dozen cop cars parked along the street, most on the right, next to the station. One car was pulling into a parking spot and another was leaving. Cops in uniform were all around, getting in and out of the cars, standing on the sidewalk, talking and laughing with their buddies.

Trudell saw them, too, but he wasn't pleased. "Jesus Christ," he said. "I'll kill you." Trudell had the gun almost against the glass, pointed at the back of Joe's head.

"Maybe," Joe said mildly, "but I wouldn't fire that little cap pistol back there. The ricochet might put out your eye."

There was a parking spot across from the station, almost exactly where Sanders had jaywalked. Joe pulled into the spot and shut off the engine.

"What the fuck are you doing?" Trudell hissed, the feedback turning it into a high pitched squeal.

Joe turned around and looked right into the barrel of the gun. "Sit back. Relax," he said. "I want to tell you a story."

CHAPTER 26

Trudell looked stunned. "You're fucking nuts," he said, but the gun that he pointed at Joe had a slight tremor.

"Yeah?" Joe shrugged. "Well, I've been called worse things, but I'm not nuts enough to risk you pulling that trigger if I didn't know this was bullet-proof glass. Okay? So why don't you put it away, just in case one of those cops comes over. It might be awkward to explain."

Trudell looked at him with a baffled expression. "I don't believe you," he muttered, but it wasn't clear what he meant. He started to put the gun back inside his coat, then thought better of it and stuffed it under the back of the seat, where it was hidden in the thick leather upholstery.

Joe smiled. "Great. Now, let me tell you how this is going to go. You don't need to do anything but listen. When we're done, I'll drop you off wherever you want to go. I hope you'll feel like taking some of my story back to whoever hired you, but I can't force you to. That's up to you."

Trudell had gained back a little confidence. "Who do you think hired me? And to do what?" he asked.

"I don't know who they are," Joe said, "and I don't want to know. I think they hired you to kill Art Delaney, and what I want you to do is to go back to them and convince them that's a bad idea."

Trudell laughed, but it sounded weak and hollow, and he gave it up quickly. "Man, you've got a vivid imagination."

"I like to think so, but I'm not imagining what you're here for. The people that hired you think they can protect themselves by killing an old man. I'm going to show you why that won't work."

Trudell glanced out at the cops coming and going across the street. None of them seemed to be paying any attention to the big black car. He sat back in the seat and shrugged. "Go ahead."

"Alright," Joe said, settling in himself. "This goes way back, back to the seventies and early eighties, when Somerville crime was still independent. There were three gangs operating back then, all ready to go to war for the top spot in the city. Of course, the national organization was just waiting for the war to be over. Then they'd come in and pick up the pieces. It's a great strategy. It's worked for centuries.

"So they sent in a guy named Bobby Coluccio. He was a scout for the Boston mob, but nobody in Somerville knew that. To them, he was just some punk from Dorchester who came in and started nosing around, asking questions. His job was to figure out which gang the Boston mob should back. They must have figured they could back a winner and make the takeover that much easier. Anyway, they sent Coluccio in to see who was strongest.

"So, one day Coluccio goes to one of the local bookies and starts asking questions, makes the guy nervous. The bookie complains to Art Delaney, who handles him for Pat Sheehan, one of the gang bosses. Sheehan tells Art to go talk to Coluccio, tell him to cut the shit. In other words, don't bother me with this shit. Handle it.

"But Art wasn't much of a tough guy. He wants back up. There's this guy hanging around, some kind of half-assed lawyer, thinks he's a hard ass. Hangs around Sheehan's gang, trying to get in on the action. Sheehan tells Art to take the guy along. They're just going to talk to Coluccio. How much fire power do they need?

"The two of them go to Coluccio's place. Coluccio's wife is out visiting a friend and Coluccio's home babysitting their two kids. Art and his backup go right up to the door and ring the bell. They start talking to Coluccio and go inside, but Coluccio's a tough punk, not intimidated at all. He knows he's got the mob behind him. Why should he worry about a couple jerks from some piss-ass local gang? He practically laughs in their face. Art tries to reason with him, but the other guy starts getting in Coluccio's face. Something happened. Coluccio pushed him or something, and the guy goes apeshit, pulls a knife and sticks it in Coluccio's neck. Coluccio drops to the floor, bleeding all over the place. Art's in shock. He never saw anything like that. He goes to help Coluccio, then decides he needs an ambulance. He goes in the kitchen to call, but he can't even find the number. He hears screams from somewhere in the house. He drops the phone and runs upstairs, but the kids are already dead, hacked up pretty bad. Art didn't even know they were in the house.

"This punk, this half assed lawyer – he's covered with blood and babbling like an idiot. Art gets him out of there and cleaned up, and he wipes down everything he can think of. By this time, the guy's quiet, acting like nothing happened. They go to Sheehan and Art tells him the whole thing. Sheehan can't believe it - a triple murder, two kids, all about a two-bit bookie, and the guy that did it is sitting there like he's a hero. Sheehan wants to kill the fucking psycho, but he can't afford that kind of problem just when things are heating up for a gang war. Art thinks they got out pretty clean, so Sheehan's got to let the guy go. All he can do is banish him from the gang.

"So Coluccio's wife comes home and finds her husband and kids dead in oceans of blood. She goes to pieces. The cops investigate, but they never figure it out."

Trudell was interested despite himself. "And the mob never found out either?" he asked.

"If they did, it was many years later, when anybody that knew Coluccio was either dead or didn't care anymore. But the point is, whether they ever found out or not, I don't think they sent you after Art for revenge."

"No?"

"No. Like I said, they're protecting someone, someone who's important to them now. It turns out the guy who actually did the killing, that half-assed lawyer - he was working for some ambulance chaser back then, but he had big ideas. He started working for this big connected real estate developer, called it lobbying. Really he was just spreading bribes around, but it got him noticed. The guys on Beacon Hill tend to like anybody who gives them money. They pushed him on the party and got his name on the ballot, so he's a state rep now. His name's Ed Reese, and he's one of the biggest politicians the mob has in its pocket."

"So you think the mob is going after Art Delaney to protect their tame politician?"

"Bet on it."

"Why now, after thirty years?"

"Coluccio's widow died about a month ago. She'd had a rough time all those years – drugs, alcohol, in and out of mental hospitals, living on the streets. Like I said, Delaney isn't very tough. He heard about the widow and it brought it all back, the memory of those kids cut up in all that blood, the guilt for what the widow went through. He couldn't handle it, started coming apart. Somebody must have seen it and decided to take preventive action."

Trudell was unimpressed. "So why should any of this make them change their minds?"

"It shouldn't. It's the fact that I know it. When Art started going to pieces, he started talking. There's already a dozen people that know that story. The cops know it. The thing is, there's not a damn thing they can do with it. If it came down to it, it's just Art's word against a state representative, an ex-con against an elected public official with a clean record. There's nothing else. It would never get to court, and even if the papers got it, it would sound like bullshit. Art can't hurt Reese, or the mob.

"But, if Art gets killed, murdered – especially by a pro like yourself – then the cops are going to open it up again for real. They've got to look into this old story, see if it's a motive. You think that won't make the papers? Even the sniff of something as dirty as that would be the kiss of death to their cozy little deal with Ed Reese. Everything he does will be under the microscope. They got to drop him like a hot potato. Right?"

"Yeah, maybe." Trudell said. "And this is the story you want me to take back to these 'people' I'm supposed to be working for?"

"That's it."

Trudell looked out at the cops and his face took on a cold, distant look. "Good. Let's go. I got things I want to do tonight."

Joe turned back to the steering wheel. "Where to, Mr. Trudell?"

CHAPTER 27

Trudell wanted to go back to the Parker House. There was no more conversation as Joe drove him there. When he pulled into the same reserved spot he'd used earlier, he pushed the button that unlocked the back doors. It made an audible click, and he turned to Trudell. "Would you mind if I don't get the door for you. I'd feel a little safer this way."

Trudell stared at him blankly for a moment before a faint smile flitted briefly across his face. "No. You're right. It is safer," he said. "But there's something we should get clear first."

Joe nodded.

Trudell went on, looking into Joe's face with a deadly serious stare. "Hijacking me to tell me this story was a risky move. If you get away with it," - he stressed the "if" – "I want you to understand it's because I'm assuming you've had your say, and you won't be causing me any more trouble. You understand what I'm saying?"

"I do," Joe nodded again. "I think, if you take this story back to whoever needs to hear it, our paths will never need to cross again."

"That would be good ..." Trudell said, "for you."

"I understand."

Trudell stuffed the gun inside his coat and got out. He walked into the Parker House without looking back.

Al Trautman was happy to see Joe drive into the lot. He was standing by the door when Joe got out of the limo. There was no one else in the lot, which was enclosed by the blank brick walls of the surrounding buildings. A floodlight was mounted on one of the walls, shedding a weak shadowy light down on the blacktop.

"See," Joe said, "no holes – in me or the car."

"That's good," Trautman nodded. "You accomplish whatever it was you wanted?"

"I don't know. I hope so."

"And Art's okay?"

"For now."

"Is he going to be back, or does he have to disappear?"

"That's what I don't know. It should be clear in the next few days, maybe sooner. Anyway, you got one of your limos upgraded. You can go into a whole new line of business."

Trautman frowned. "I'm not sure I want a business where I've got to protect my drivers from their clients."

"That's true. You want this suit? I've already got one for weddings and funerals."

"Why not. I'll keep it around. Might not fit any of my current drivers, but you never know."

Joe walked into the dispatch office with Trautman. "You know, it'd probably be best if you kept all this quiet for awhile. I don't know if anybody will come around asking questions, but I don't think it's over yet. If it's the cops, you've got to tell them what you know, but with anyone else, tell them nothing and call me. I'll be sure to show my usual appreciation."

Trautman grinned. "Sounds good to me."

Joe changed into his jeans and sweatshirt and took the T back to Davis. It was only a little past 10:00. He was tired, but he didn't go straight home. He knew he'd have to deal with Chad Reese again, and that Chad could be waiting at his place at that very moment. But it wasn't fear that made him stop in at the Town Tavern before he went home; it was something more like battle fatigue. He was tired of the stress of confrontation. A couple beers, some bullshitting with some of the regulars, catch the Bruins recap – maybe then he'd feel a little more like plodding ahead.

He went in and sat at the bar next to Al Mathews. Al was watching the big flat screen TV on the wall behind the bar, where two ex-hockey players were discussing the game with an attractive young blond. Al looked over at Joe when he climbed onto the stool.

"Hey Joe," he greeted him, "you catch the game?"

"No. I was busy."

"You didn't miss much. They blew a lead in the third period, tried to sit on it, let the Islanders walk all over them. The Islanders, for chrissakes."

Tim brought Joe a beer. On the screen, the announcers wrapped up for a commercial break. Al downed what was left of his beer.

"See you, Joe," he said, getting off his stool. "I got to get home. The wife won't let me watch the game on my own TV, but she'll cut my balls off if I'm not home the minute it's over."

"Yeah," Joe smiled, "see you, Al."

Joe stared at the TV, where the commercials blared and flashed. All around him, the bar was full of sound and motion, but he wasn't aware of any of it. Al's mention of his wife reminded him he was supposed to call Eileen when he was done with his business. It set off an odd game of mental ping pong in his head.

The business was done. But his cell phone was dead. Tim had a phone he could use. But there'd be all that bar noise in the background. Eileen would be turned off. But this was where he wanted to be. Let her be turned off. He had to be who he was. And she had to see it.

He asked Tim for the phone and dialed her number.

"Hello," he heard her say.

"Hi."

"Joe," she said eagerly. "I've been waiting for you to call. Is everything alright?"

"Yeah. Yeah, I guess so. What are you up to?"

She gave a strangled laugh. "Not much. I'm trying to read a patent application, but I can't concentrate. Can we get together tonight?"

"Um, yeah, but could you come in here? I'm kind of worn out."

"That'd be fine. But ... where are you? What's all that noise?"

"I'm at the Town Tavern. I stopped in after I was done with my ... errands."

"Oh. Do you want me to come there?"

Joe looked around at the rough crowd and laughed softly to himself. He felt the knot in his stomach start to relax. "No. I'll meet you at my place."

Joe poured the rest of his beer down his throat and got down off the stool. He had a vague smile on his face as he walked out the door. He was thinking, "Wrong again."

CHAPTER 28

The intercom buzzed. A tinny voice said, "Mr. Reese, your son Chad is here to see you. Shall I send him up?"

Ed Reese pushed a button next to the shiny brass speaker set into the wall. "Send him up, Virgil."

The senior Reese was of medium height and slight build. He had a full head of neatly trimmed salt-and-pepper hair, and his narrow face had sagged very little. He wore gray dress slacks and a powder blue dress shirt, open at the neck.

A minute or two later, he heard the ding of the elevator arriving at his floor. There was a knock at the door to his apartment. Reese opened it and Chad walked in. He moved with a slow, stiff-legged gait. Ed shut the door and watched Chad hobble down the short hall.

"Still hurting, huh?" he said without much sympathy.

An angry grunt was the only response.

Ed followed Chad into the living room, a broad expanse of blond wood floor, surrounded by white walls and ceiling, with rectangular, black and white, modern furniture arrayed around a thick carpet in which swaths of purple, scarlet and gold wound around each other. It all looked out, through a wall of windows, across the roofs of Back Bay town houses, across the Charles River, to the lighted shores of Cambridge.

"You want a drink?" Ed asked. "You look like you could use it."

"Yeah," Chad said, lowering himself gently onto the sofa, "I could."

Ed went into the kitchen and fixed drinks for the two of them. Chad lay back and let his head rest on the low back of the sofa. He closed his eyes and breathed deeply.

Ed came back into the room and put a coaster on the glass top coffee table. He put a short glass on the coaster and sat in a leather chair across from his son. He took a sip of his own drink and watched Chad with a worried frown.

"I don't like this," he said. "It's a risk with Polito out there, running around loose."

"God damn it," Chad growled. "What could go wrong? If Trudell's any good, it's a piece of cake."

"Just like tailing Polito was a piece of cake."

Chad sat up, snarling. "That fucking Sanders. He's the one that fucked that up."

"Yeah, but you didn't do so hot with it, either. Polito is slick. If he sticks his nose in Trudell's business, we could be in deep shit."

Chad sipped his drink. "Quit worrying. Nothing's going to go wrong. Anyway, when this business with Delaney is done, I want Trudell to take out Polito."

Ed was silent for a moment, staring at Chad who glared right back. He shook his head. "It's not going to happen," he said flatly. "I called in a favor to deal with Delaney. I don't have enough credit for another."

"What the fuck," Chad blazed. "The deals you're bringing in, they can't keep their guy here another day or two? Bullshit."

"You don't get it. I'm only an asset as long as I'm a respected politician. As soon as there's any stink around me, I become an instant liability. I don't even want to think what they do with a liability."

"What stink? Polito's got no connection to you."

"No, but he's got one with you and Art Delaney. And who knows who he's talking to. You don't know these guys. They're careful. They don't take chances.

This thing with Delaney was bad enough. I claimed he was trying to bleed me for some old business from the Somerville days, penny ante shit but enough to embarrass me. They bought it, but they don't like it. I go back for another, they're going to be asking questions, serious questions, questions I can't answer. I'm not getting into that."

Chad heard the finality in his father's voice, and he knew enough not to argue, but the issue of Polito was not over for him. It would never be over until Polito was dead.

Chad watched the Bruins game with his father, but they were both on edge, and the game was not enough to distract them. It was something to do while they waited for the call that would confirm the completion of Trudell's mission. Ed thought the call would come some time between 9:30 and midnight, depending on how it went. He was not surprised when the game ended and the call had not yet come. They had another drink and watched the wrap up.

The call came just after 10:30.

Ed took it. "Hello?" he said in a flat, mechanical voice, attempting to mask the urgency he felt. After that, he said nothing more for a long, agonizing minute. Chad watched his face and quickly saw that the news was not good.

"Can't we take another shot?" Ed finally said.

"... no, but ..." he was cut off.

There was another long pause.

"Yeah, he's right here."

"... I know, but ..."

"Yeah, okay," Ed said, and hung up.

He laid the phone down gently on the coffee table. His face was clouded as he looked up at Chad.

"Delaney didn't show. They sent some other driver and Trudell had to ride around for an hour before he could claim a change of plans and get back to George."

"Shit." Chad's face was blank as he tried to digest it. "What are they going to do now?"

Ed Reese looked disgusted. "Nothing. Trudell's going home, and George says he won't put the organization in a compromising position for some old dirt."

Chad was stunned. "But what if Delaney goes to the cops?"

"You don't get it," Ed flared. "If Delaney goes to the cops, they lose me; so they find somebody else to carry their water at the State House. If they get caught in a murder conspiracy, the whole thing comes down. They're not going to risk it. We're on our own."

"Shit."

"That's what he said." Ed lay back in his chair with a weary sigh. "He said to tell you it was a good plan, but shit happens."

"Yeah," Chad snorted contemptuously. "That's fine for him, but we're left swinging in the wind. I thought these guys took care of their own."

Ed looked out across the river. His face was distorted by bitterness and fear. "That's the problem," he said. "We're not their own."

"Well, what the fuck do we do? We can't let Delaney run around loose."

"No," Ed said, going over the brief call in his head. Nothing George had said could be construed as a threat, but there had been a cool distance in the tone. Ed knew what that meant. "No," he repeated, "we can't."

When Chad left the apartment around midnight, they had a plan. Ed didn't like it, but there wasn't much they could do until they smoked Art Delaney out of hiding. Chad was satisfied. Their plan put him one on one with Polito, and he was already anticipating the satisfaction of seeing Polito gasping out his last breath, choking on his own blood.

Chad took the elevator down to the parking garage beneath the building. He didn't see Sanders, who was waiting near the Charger. Nor did he notice the little green Toyota that followed him all the way back to his apartment in Charlestown.

CHAPTER 29

Joe thought he knew how a guy like Chad Reese would respond to the kind of beating Joe had given him, and he knew he'd to have to face him again. He had an irrational trust that the law would back him when the time came, and he was looking forward to it. When he got back to his house, he did a quick check of the street before he went in. There was no one sitting in a parked car, no one walking the street or freezing his ass off, lurking in the bushes. For the moment, that was good enough. Joe went inside, and Eileen arrived a few minutes later.

They went into his tiny kitchen, where Joe poured the Blanton's into glasses. "How's Jake?" he asked.

"I don't know," Eileen sighed. "He went to bed without a fuss, but he seemed kind of withdrawn, like he knows there's something wrong, but he doesn't know what. It makes him angry and afraid."

"I don't blame him," Joe muttered, "but I think his grandfather is okay for now."

"What do you mean? What did you find out?"

"Art wasn't just hiding from a guilty conscience. There were people out to get him. I might have changed their minds about that tonight."

They went into Joe's living room and sat together on the sofa. Without going into detail, he told her about relaying his message through Trudell.

Eileen frowned. "But why would they want to kill him?"

"Because he knew about a crime from way back, before he went to prison. They were afraid he might start talking and mess up their current business."

"How could something from thirty years ago be so important?"

Joe looked down into the honey colored liquor that he held in his glass. "They never close the book on murder," he said softly, "especially when the victims are kids."

"Kids?" she groaned. "Oh, my god. What did my father have to do with that?"

"Like he told Jake, he was there. He saw it. That's what's been eating away at him."

"Oh god," she sighed. "How awful. But you think they'll leave him alone now?"

"I don't know. I'd like to think I shook up the hornets' nest. What comes out, we'll just have to wait and see."

"You mean there's nothing more we can do?"

"Not much. I'm going to try to catch up with Pat Sheehan and Art tomorrow. I don't know if I'll have any luck, but I'd like to talk to Art and find out what he wants to do. It was Art's conscience that started all this. It's not going to be done until that's put to rest."

They were both silent for a moment. Then Joe said, "I still think it would be good for you to talk to him, too."

Her face was bleak, turned to the window. "I know. I've thought about it endlessly, but I don't know what I could say. Everything I think of sounds so hollow, like a cliché."

"But you're his daughter. You're closer to him than anybody."

"No." She shook her head emphatically. "Jake is close to him. Art and I are still strangers. I don't really know him."

She looked into Joe's eyes for something, some sign of understanding, or even disgust. But there was nothing, just a searching look that seemed to peer down inside her. She shrank from it, ashamed.

"I ... I guess that's awful, isn't it – my own father."

Joe sipped his drink thoughtfully. "Yeah, it's awful, but not so unusual. I think a lot of people have trouble staying close to their parents when they're adults."

"What about your parents, Joe? Are you close to them?"

"They're dead."

"Oh. I'm sorry."

Joe shrugged. "Nothing to be sorry about. If you asked them, they'd say they did alright, even though they didn't make a pile of money and they both died young."

"It's funny. I think Art's kind of like that. Until this stuff came up out of the past, he seemed very content with his life. He was just a step up from being homeless, and he spent all that time in prison. I guess it doesn't really matter what you do. It's how you feel about it that counts."

"True."

"And that's my problem. No matter what I do, I don't feel anything."

"What about Jake?"

Eileen looked away. "I don't know. Anna's really more of a mother to him than I am. I'd do anything for him, but I can't really say why. Is it because I love him with a mother's natural love? Or is it because I feel guilty that I don't have that love inside me and I'm trying to make up for it? I've asked myself that question a thousand times, and I just don't know the answer."

Joe didn't know the answer, either, so he said nothing.

"Remember last night," Eileen continued, "you said it's only when you see through all the stuff of my life – the job, the house, the money – only when you can see through all that that you like what you see?"

"Yeah."

"What's there? What do you see?" she asked, the pain trembling in her voice. "When I look past all that stuff, I'm not sure I see anything at all."

Joe took his time trying to figure out a way to tell her the truth without hurting her any more, but he finally had to just say it. "What I see is a person in there, struggling to get out. The fact that you're asking these questions shows me that. Like I said, there's a lot of things in the way, and I can't really tell who that person is, or if she'll ever climb out." He made a weak laugh. "But I know you're in there somewhere."

"You're the only one, Joe," she said with a catch in her voice. "You're the only one who sees that. That's why I need you so much."

She pulled him to her and kissed him with all the fear and desperation he had seen in her face the first time they made love.

CHAPTER 30

Eileen stayed the night, and Joe did not wake up until 7:30 – late for him. When he opened his eyes, Eileen was curled up facing him. The innocence of sleep smoothed her features making her look younger and more beautiful than Joe had ever seen her. He got quietly out of bed, pulled on his jeans and sweatshirt, cranked up the heat, and put the coffee pot on the burner.

Ten minutes later, he woke her up. "There's coffee, if you want it."

Eileen rolled over and smiled up at him. "I'd love some."

He was standing beside the bed with two cups in his hands. She sat up, and he handed her one. "Sorry, I don't have any milk."

"That's okay. I drink it black."

She took a sip. "Ooh, that's strong. Maybe a little sugar."

"Oh, yeah." Joe went into the kitchen and brought out a little bowl of sugar and a teaspoon, which he put on the nightstand for her.

Eileen laughed. "Wow. I think I'd like to wake up here every day."

"No you wouldn't," Joe said lightly. "What about Jake?"

"That's true. We'd need a room for him."

"We wouldn't want to shock him."

She looked at the twisted blankets and sheets with a smug grin. "We are rather shocking, aren't we?"

"I think it's you," Joe teased. "Usually I'm much more refined."

Jake had hockey practice that morning, so Eileen had some time, and she meant to enjoy it. When they finished their coffee, she got Joe back into bed for another round of love-making. Joe was a bit concerned that he had nothing left, but Eileen was so fresh and eager, he managed to rise to the occasion.

They walked up to the sandwich shop and had eggs and sausage and pancakes. Joe was astonished at her appetite. He'd seen her naked, and there wasn't an ounce of fat on her body. Yet she ordered a massive breakfast and ate every bit of it, including the little slice of orange that Joe had always thought was just for show.

"That's a great little place," she said as they left.

Joe was glancing up at the park, casually trying to spot a tail if there was one. "Yeah," he said. "It's mostly for the Tufts kids, but they don't kick me out."

It was a beautiful winter morning; the air was clean, cold and dry. The sky was bright blue, and much of the salt and sand that had been spread over the streets and sidewalks had washed into the gutters. Joe scanned the park for any sign of a tail while Eileen chattered happily. He kept her going with a word here and there and wondered at her mood, so dark the night before and now so light-hearted. Both moods seemed honest and unforced, and he decided that neither invalidated the other. Maybe this ability to flash from one outlook to another was a natural protective mechanism, a way for our hearts and minds to maintain a balance and keep the poisons from building up inside. The lack of that balance in the characters of his Russian novel was probably what made them so fascinating, but it also made them somewhat unreal.

As they turned onto Morrison, Joe's cell phone chirped from his pocket. He looked at the number and didn't recognize it.

"Hello?"

"Polito, it's me, Pat Sheehan." The voice was hoarse and exhausted. "I see you're still alive. How'd it go last night?"

"Good. I got my message delivered, and, like you say, I'm still here. How about you? You and Art find a comfortable place to spend the night?"

Sheehan laughed briefly. "We did alright."

"So what's next?" Joe asked bluntly. "You bringing Art home?"

"I don't know yet. There's a couple things I got to find out first."

"When? When will you know?"

"Today, I hope. This running around, babysitting a crazy old man is wearing me down."

"When you figure it out, will you let me know?"

"You'll be the first."

Joe snapped the phone off.

"That was Pat Sheehan?" Eileen asked. The light-hearted tone was gone.

"Yeah," Joe said absently.

"What are they doing?"

"He didn't tell me, but they seem like they're doing okay."

"Doesn't it seem a little crazy, a couple old men running around the city, trying to keep out of sight?"

Joe smiled. "Yeah, but I think your father's in pretty good hands. Sheehan's old and sick, but he's still sharp, and he knows the people he's dealing with. That and the fact that he feels like he owes Art a lot. Art would be in deep shit without him."

"I guess," she said doubtfully, "but I wish he'd let me help him."

"I'm sure that's the last thing he wants – to let his mistakes pull you and Jake into this shit."

"I don't think there was any way to avoid it."

"No," Joe agreed, "probably not."

Joe was relieved when they got back to his place and Eileen said she had to go home. She could be a complication if she was with him when he met up with Reese. He stood beside her car and kissed her goodbye, telling her he'd call if he heard from Art or Pat Sheehan. She drove away and Joe went into his house. Chad watched all this from his vantage up the street. He let Eileen go and stuck with Polito.

Joe paid some bills the old-fashioned way, with a check and a stamp. He put the envelopes in a stack on the corner of his desk and moved to his chair, where he picked up his book and tried to read. But again, he was antsy. The business with Art wasn't finished, and there was nothing he could do about it at the moment. Reese was out there somewhere, waiting to bash his brains out. Joe would have loved to get going with that, but the next move was up to Reese. He decided to go for a run, and he was about to change into his sweats, when his phone went off. It was Eileen.

"Hi," he said.

"Joe, Jake went off with Art this morning." Her voice was choked with tension. "They're at the science museum."

"What?"

"When I got home, Anna told me Jake had called and said he was going to a friend's house. His friend's mom would pick them up from hockey practice. I didn't think anything of it. Jake's done that lots of times. But it was Art that picked him up

184

– Art and Pat Sheehan, evidently. I just got a call from Art, and he admitted he put Jake up to the lie."

"Why the science museum?"

"Jake picked it. He's been on a kick with dinosaurs and prehistoric life since they covered it in school. The museum has all kinds of dinosaur exhibits. I've been meaning to take him myself."

"So Jake and Art planned this?"

"Evidently. Art said he knew how upset Jake was after his call yesterday and it wasn't the way he wanted him to remember his grandfather."

"He's still talking like it's goodbye."

"Yes," she said slowly, "but he wasn't being dramatic. He seemed to know exactly what he wanted."

"Huh," Joe said, taking a moment to think about it. "Maybe that's a good thing. He's been unsure about it for a long time."

"Maybe, but what about Jake. If they're still after Art, isn't it dangerous for Jake to be with him."

"I doubt it. Remember, that was the problem in the first place. These guys don't like to take it out on the families, and especially not the kids."

"I hope you're right." She sounded nervous, uncertain. "Anyway, I've got to go. I told him I'd meet them in half an hour. I guess the reason I called is I was hoping you'd come too. I'd feel better."

"Sure," Joe said. "I've been looking for this guy for days. I'm not going to drop out now, just when we're about to find him."

CHAPTER 31

Joe said he'd meet her at the ticket booths in half an hour. He took the subway to Charles Street and walked from there. If he hadn't had to wait 10 minutes for a train, he would have been early. As it was, he walked through the front entrance into the foyer of the Museum of Science just as Eileen came down the hall from the parking garage. There were dozens of people milling around in the foyer, lines at the ticket booths, the noise of a many conversations, all the distracting sensations of a busy public place, but she spotted him immediately and hurried over.

"Joe," she said as they met in the middle of the wide marble hall. "Thanks for coming."

"I wanted to," Joe said, looking around. "I haven't seen Art yet. Have you?"

"No. I just got here."

"They were going to meet you out here?"

"Yes. Maybe we're a few minutes early."

"Wait. There's Pat Sheehan." Unconsciously he held her hand as he led her through the crowd to a marble bench along the wall.

Sheehan was sitting on the bench, leaning back against the wall. He looked shrunken in clothes that must have fit when he bought them. His eyes were closed and his face was pale, with bright spots standing out on his cheeks. They could hear the rough hiss of his breathing as his chest moved up and down.

"Pat," Joe said sharply.

Sheehan opened his eyes and looked at them without expression. "Yeah."

"This is Art's daughter, Eileen Merrill." Joe seemed embarrassed, but he turned to Eileen to complete the introduction. "Eileen, this is Pat Sheehan."

Eileen took a step toward him and smiled a tentative smile. "Hello Mr. Sheehan. It's nice to see you again."

Joe looked at her with a puzzled frown.

Pat Sheehan did not seem surprised. His lips curled into a faint smile, and he sat up and looked at her. "So you're little Eileen Delaney. I haven't seen you since you were seven years old. I'm surprised you remember me."

"Oh, you made a big impression. I think it was a wedding reception, right? You were so tall, and everybody seemed to gather around you, and you bent down to shake my hand. I knew you were a very important person."

Sheehan's smile turned wry and a little sour. "Back then, I thought so too."

"Are you waiting for Art?" Eileen asked.

"Mostly I was waiting for you. I've been driving your old man all over town, and I'm beat. I don't know if I can still stand up." He looked from her to Joe. "You've got to take over, now."

"Of course," she said quickly. "And I want to thank you for helping my father. I'm sure it wasn't easy."

"Art's done his best not to make it easy, but you don't need to thank me. Art's a friend. As long as I'm breathing I'm going to do what I can for him."

Joe saw Art and a dark haired boy making their way through the crowd. Art was a small man with gray hair, fine features and mild blue eyes. He wore brown cotton pants and a baggy gray sweater. The fine features had been passed all the way down to Jake, but not the blue eyes. His were dark and lively.

187

They both looked a little sheepish and uncertain as they approached.

"Here he is," Joe said, "the fugitive."

Eileen hadn't yet seen them. When she turned, they were standing in front of her.

"Hi Mom," Jake said tentatively.

Eileen exhaled a sigh and shook her head, but her eyes weren't angry. "Art, you should have told me. I ..."

"I know," the old man said. "I've made a lot of trouble for everyone. I didn't mean to."

"Of course not." Eileen's tone was forgiving. "I know what you've been dealing with. I know how hard that must be."

Art frowned. "You know."

"Joe told me."

Art turned to Joe. "Hello Joe."

Joe said, "She had to know."

"Oh, I know. I just wish I'd had the courage to tell her myself."

There was an uncomfortable silence. Jake looked around at all the adults, who seemed unable to meet his eyes.

"Mom," he said, "can me and Grandpa go back in. I didn't get to see the exhibit about how life started on earth, and I really want to. Just a half hour ... please."

Eileen looked to Joe. He shrugged. "I don't think it would be a problem."

"Alright," she said with a little forced brightness, "I'll go too. Just let me buy a ticket. Would anybody else like to come?"

"Not me," Sheehan said quickly. "And Joe, maybe you could stay here. There's a couple things I'd like to talk over with you."

"Yeah, okay. I'll catch that exhibit some other time."

Art, Eileen and Jake went over to the ticket booth and waited in line, while Joe sat down next to Pat on the bench. Just outside the big glass doors, Chad slid his cell phone into his jacket pocket. He had watched the little family reunion and called his father the moment Art Delaney appeared. Ed Reese was on his way to the science museum.

Sheehan leaned back against the wall and took a few deep, noisy breaths. He was tired and weak, but his mind and will were still strong. Joe knew he had something to say. He sat beside him on the bench and waited to hear it.

"I called my contact in the Boston organization," Pat said. "Your message got through."

"What'd they think?" Joe asked.

"They agreed with you. Reese isn't worth the risk."

"Did they know about Coluccio?"

"Didn't seem like it, but they'd never say one way or the other. You can't get a straight answer out of these guys anymore. It's like they got a lawyer sitting on their lap, telling them what to say. They're so god damn careful."

"If they didn't know about it, did they care?"

"I doubt it. Ancient history. It's just business now. Coluccio was written off years ago."

"So Art's in the clear."

"I didn't say that. The organization cancelled the hit, but that doesn't mean Reese is going to let him go his merry way. Reese has been driving this from the start, and having the mob pull out just ups the pressure."

"How's that?"

"If they're not backing him anymore because he looks like he could fall in some smelly shit, they're probably not far from shutting him down for good, just so they don't get splashed. I don't think he's stupid. I think he knows that."

"Oh," Joe said, suddenly seeing the cold, clear logic of it.

"No, I don't think Ed Reese is feeling all that comfortable right now. And the only way he gets comfortable is to show them the risk isn't that bad. That means getting rid of Art ... and me, and probably you, and maybe even Art's little girl."

"You think he'd do that?" Joe asked incredulously.

"He killed two kids in cold blood, didn't he? Who says he's changed?"

"So, what do you think we should do?"

"It's not 'we' anymore. I got to go home and die. Anyway, Art's made up his mind. When his daughter and grandson go home, he's going to the cops and tell them the whole story. At this point, it's probably his only option. Otherwise, Ed Reese is going to find a way to take him out."

CHAPTER 32

Half an hour later, Sheehan was resting, his back propped against the wall, his eyes closed. Joe saw Art, Jake and Eileen crossing the marble floor toward him, and he studied the family dynamics. Jake walked between Art and his mother. He and Art seemed to be carrying on a lively conversation, glancing at each other, talking and laughing. Eileen did not seem to be involved. She walked beside them, looking preoccupied and vaguely worried, apparently absorbed in her own thoughts.

Joe stood up as they approached. He smiled at Jake. "How was the exhibit?"

"Cool."

"Very cool," Art agreed.

Eileen smiled.

"Ready to go?" Joe asked.

"I'm ready," Art said, and Joe knew he meant he was ready for more than just the drive home.

Sheehan sat up and took a deep rasping breath. "Somebody help me up."

Joe gave him a hand and pulled him to his feet. He was light, but he had no strength of his own. He put a hand on Joe's shoulder for support, and the whole group made their way slowly down the long hallway to the parking garage. If Joe had not been concentrating on matching his pace to Pat Sheehan's slow, unsteady shuffle, he might have noticed the Reeses trying to blend into the crowd, following behind them.

At the end of the hall, Joe's group got in the elevator. Chad had to run down the hall and bolt up the stairs, stopping at each landing to see if they got off at that level. At the fourth floor, he peered through the little glass window in the stairwell door and saw them slowly moving down an aisle of parked cars. He called his father and gave him the floor, then watched until the group was nearly out of sight, before he made a move to follow.

It was cold in the garage. There were only a few people on the big, dimly lit concrete floor, all moving purposefully to and from their cars. Chad walked in the direction the group had taken, watching over the tops of the parked cars to be sure they didn't suddenly appear and spot him. He stopped just short of the aisle down which they had turned and peered carefully around an SUV.

They were standing near the tail of a black Lincoln about six cars down the aisle. Art Delaney was saying something to the tall sickly looking old man that his father had told him was Pat Sheehan, the notorious former leader of the Somerville mob. Chad had heard the stories of Sheehan's reign, the body count and the tightly knit organization that took care of its widows and orphans, but he found it hard to believe this feeble stick was the same man.

He also knew that this was the man that had dismissed his father as an embarrassment. His father had pulled off one of the biggest killings of the gang war – the one that started it all – and Sheehan had banished him like a diseased whore. That, and his personal issue with Polito- the ache in his groin that the run up the stairs had reawakened – it all added up to a lot of vengeance to be had, standing just fifty feet away.

Delaney kept talking, and every second added to the jumping twitch of Chad's nerves. He listened impatiently for the sound of his father's car coming up the ramp. At any moment, the group would pile into the Lincoln and drive away, leaving Chad standing among the cars with nothing but a license number and a loaded gun. If his father did not bring up the car in time, they would lose the tail before it began.

Suddenly Delaney hugged Pat Sheehan and Chad realized they were saying goodbye. That meant they were leaving in more than one car. The plan he and his father had put together was falling apart, and it could easily be their last chance. Art, Eileen, and Jake turned to walk away, as Joe began to help Pat Sheehan into the big black car. Chad felt a panicky need to do something quick and decisive.

He stepped out from behind the SUV and advanced toward them. There was a pistol in his right hand, but it wasn't pointed at anyone. "Wait," he said, loudly. "Art Delaney – all of you – get back over here."

Art turned and looked at him with a puzzled frown that quickly turned to shock and fear when he saw the gun. He stepped tentatively in front of Eileen, who instinctively grabbed Jake and pulled him close to her.

Joe quickly moved around the Lincoln, back into the aisle, facing Chad, who had stopped about 10 feet away. "What do you want, Reese?"

Pat Sheehan hobbled out behind him, supporting himself with a hand on the trunk of the car. "Reese," he laughed. "You're Ed Reese's kid?"

Chad hesitated. "I'm Officer Chad Reese," he said, trying to muster some authority, "and I'm taking you all in for questioning."

A gray mid-size Toyota moved slowly across the opening at the end of the aisle and stopped suddenly. It backed up, pulled into the aisle, and stopped. Ed Reese got out and left the engine running.

"What are you doing?" he whispered urgently as he approached Chad.

"I need to take these people in for questioning. I think they have knowledge about a murder, and they've been conspiring to withhold it."

Ed stared at him without comprehension.

Pat Sheehan laughed, but it sounded more like a rasping cough. "Bullshit," he said. "You're not taking us anywhere."

He took a step away from the car, a step closer to Chad. With another step, he stood in front of Joe. It took a great effort, and he seemed to totter on his feet.

"Stop right there," Chad said, raising the gun.

"You're out of your jurisdiction," Pat growled hoarsely." Show me a shield." He took another shaky step toward Chad.

"I said to stay where you are." Panic had invaded Chad's voice. His gun wandered around, trying to threaten all of them, but they watched more with morbid fascination than with fear.

None of them moved except Sheehan. He took another short, uncertain step toward Chad. "What are you going to do?" he asked, "shoot me? That would be very messy. Wouldn't it, Ed? You couldn't get away with it. And that's the whole point, isn't it?"

Ed Reese whispered something, but Chad shook him off, again waving the gun around to indicate the whole group. "No," he shouted. "You're coming with us."

"No," Joe broke in. "Pat's right. It's not going to work, Chad. We're not going with you, and there's nothing you can do about it. Look around. We're in a public place. You've already scared two or three people out of here. They're calling the cops right now.

You're not getting out. The only question is whether you want a murder charge tacked on."

Sheehan took another step forward. He was only a couple paces in front of Chad, but he wasn't much of a threat. He looked like he might fall over on his own at any moment. Still, Chad had the gun centered on his middle.

"He's right, Chad," his father said aloud. "Put it away and let's go. We'll let the lawyers sort it out."

"No," Chad burst out. "You said ..." But he couldn't finish. He was confused. It wasn't working out the way he thought it would. The gun wasn't making any difference.

"See," Sheehan said, "even your father learned. Are you going to be a stupid punk like he was?" He took another step forward and put out his hand. "Give me the gun."

"Fuck you," Chad yelled and pulled the trigger.

The blast was incredibly loud in the garage of concrete and steel. A small flash was visible from the muzzle of the gun. Sheehan collapsed, holding his stomach. He didn't make a sound, but put out a hand to cushion his fall onto the hard concrete.

"Run," Joe shouted, ducking back behind the trunk of the Lincoln.

Art began to push Jake and Eileen into the shelter of the parked cars, but another voice rang out sharply. "Reese! Drop the gun."

Chad turned toward the sound, the gun following his line of sight, but he didn't get a chance to fire. There was a soft popping sound and Chad was knocked backwards. The gun skittered under a car. Chad lay on the concrete deck, still except for a hand that trembled spasmodically. Ed Reese looked down at him and peed in his pants.

Joe ran around the line of cars to where Art and his family were crouched out of the line of fire. Eileen was kneeling on the concrete, holding Jake in her arms. She was making faint moaning sounds and Jake seemed to be in shock. Art was wide eyed, trying to peer over the trunk of a car to see what was going on. There were no more shots, but Joe could hear vague sounds, clipped hushed voices and scuffling footsteps, from the scene of the gunfight. He didn't have time to check out whatever was happening out there.

"Get out of here," he hissed to Eileen. "Get to your car and go. Go back to Lexington and stay there. If anyone comes near that you don't know, call the police. I'll get there as soon as I can."

Car doors slammed and a car moved away. The sounds seemed natural in the resounding garage. When the noise of the car receded, it left a hollow silence.

"Joe," Eileen pleaded, "stay with us. I'm scared. What's going on?"

"I'm not sure, but the best thing is to get out of here. I'm going to help Pat if I can."

"There's nothing you can do. He got shot."

"I don't think it killed him. I've got to see if there's anything I can do. Now go."

Art grabbed her arm. "Joe's right. We've got to get Jake out of here."

He pulled her up into a crouch, keeping low behind the cars. Jake's eyes were glazed in a fixed expression, but he held his mother's hand and imitated her duck walk out to the next aisle, where Art peered around the cars before leading them in the direction of Eileen's Lexus.

Joe took Art's vantage point and lifted his eyes carefully over the trunk, to see what was happening.

Chad's body was right where it fell and very still. Pat had not moved, either, but his chest was heaving up and down with labored breathing. Ed Reese and his car were gone, and there was no sign of whoever shot Chad Reese.

He pulled the cell phone from his pocket and dialed 911, just in case no one else had. He reported the shootings and asked for an ambulance. The dispatcher wanted to keep him on the line after he'd given all the relevant information, but Joe politely hung up in order to make a call to Eileen's cell phone. She answered from the Lexus, on Storrow Drive, just passing Kenmore Square. Joe asked to talk to Art, who quickly gave him the answer he needed. Finally, he called Paul Shea, hoping to have at least one friendly face among the cops who would soon be swarming like flies around the bodies and the blood.

CHAPTER 33

The first wails of the sirens were floating up to the fourth level of the garage when Joe went over to where Pat Sheehan lay. Joe's eyes checked nervously among the parked cars for any more shooters but found none. Sheehan was on his back, his breathing ragged and noisy. His shirt had a wide dark stain along his left side. As Joe approached, his eyes were open and seemed to track him.

Joe knelt beside him. "Pat?" he asked, surprised that it was even a question.

"Yeah," Sheehan groaned.

"How bad?"

"Bad enough." His face contorted with the pain of forming words.

"There should be an ambulance in a minute."

"Okay. But, if I can't … Explain it to Rose. Okay? Tell her why."

"I will."

Sheehan took a deep shuddering breath and closed his eyes.

The cops approached the scene carefully and by the book. They had Joe put his hands on his head and patted him down. When they were satisfied that he was not an immediate threat, the garage quickly filled with uniformed professionals. The ambulance crew started carefully loading Sheehan onto a stretcher, while two cops stood with Joe, waiting for the detectives. Other cops were setting up tape in a wide perimeter around the place near the trunk of the Lincoln where Chad Reese and Pat Sheehan had been shot. Someone set up some portable lights on stands to augment the dim parking garage lighting.

Just as they were loading Pat into the back of the ambulance, one of the EMTs came over to Joe and the two uniformed cops who had just finished taking down his identification.

"The patient is asking for this one," he said to the cops, nodding at Joe.

"He can't go," one of the cops said.

"Just a word, he said."

Joe looked at the cop. "Might help you figure out what happened."

The cop was young. He looked at his partner, who shrugged.

"Okay, come on," the young one decided. They all walked over to the stretcher and stood at the open rear door of the ambulance. Sheehan's eyes were closed in a grimace of pain.

"Pat," Joe said. The cops stood close beside him, dutifully listening in on whatever passed between him and Sheehan.

Sheehan opened his eyes and gasped through gritted teeth, "They took Ed. Art's in the clear."

"Who? Who did?"

"Mob guys."

Sheehan closed his eyes and the EMTs got the stretcher into the ambulance, which immediately pulled away with its lights flashing.

The detectives arrived, Arbitus and Connally. Arbitus was short, with dark hair and eyes, and he did all the talking. Connally occasionally scribbled something into a little spiral notebook. He was six inches taller than Arbitus with curly hair and his expressionless face never changed.

Joe told them what happened, walking around the scene, pointing out the positions of the participants. Arbitus asked a few questions, but mostly let Joe tell it his way. His eyebrows went up when Joe named

Ed Reese and identified him specifically as the state rep and father of the dead Somerville cop. Otherwise, he had no comment.

Just as Joe was telling Arbitus about the calls he made following the shootings, Paul Shea showed up with a Somerville detective. Shea introduced himself and Detective Rossetti, and asked if they could participate in questioning the witnesses, based on their understanding that the shootings were connected with an unsolved murder in their jurisdiction. Arbitus seemed pleased to include them, and Connally had no reaction.

"Let's go over to the station," Arbitus suggested. "We'll be more comfortable, and we can record it there."

Joe had been in the Cambridge station many years before, and it hadn't changed much. Arbitus asked him if he would allow a technician to collect a sample from his hands and clothes to be used in a gunshot residue test. Joe had no objection and the technician took the sample in less than two minutes. Then Arbitus led Joe and Paul Shea to a small conference room, where they spent the next three hours going over everything that led up to the shooting in painful detail. Arbitus asked Joe to fill in as much of the background and motivation as he could – even if it was hearsay or pure speculation. Joe knew what he told them about the murder of Bobby Coluccio and his kids could send Art to prison, but Art had told him to go ahead and tell it. By that time, Joe figured Connally and the Somerville detective probably had Art in the next room, telling the same story anyway. The only element of the story that Joe withheld was his personal relationship with Eileen Merrill. He got the impression that Arbitus might have guessed, but let him get away with it as long as he believed it was not relevant to the case.

When they were done, Arbitus took Joe and Paul Shea down the hall to another conference room, to join Art, Eileen, and the other detectives for a group session. They all sat at a big table, looking more like a board meeting than a police interrogation. Arbitus led the questioning, which produced a strong consensus that they all might have been killed if Chad had not been shot by the unseen gunman.

"But we didn't know he was there," Art said, choking up. "Pat took the bullet so the rest of us would have a chance to get away."

They were all getting tired. The questions were starting to seem morbid and the walls of the windowless conference room began to press in around them. Eileen was silent, withdrawn. Joe and Art answered the detectives' questions patiently, but the adrenaline jag of the shootings had tailed off into a sick and restless lethargy that affected all of them. Arbitus decided to wind it up.

He stood at the head of the table and addressed Art with the bottom line. "Mr. Delaney, what you did in helping Ed Reese get away with those murders all those years ago was a crime. However, the District Attorney has elected not to file charges at this time."

Art was shocked. He looked over at Eileen and frowned a question. She gave him a weak smile and shrugged.

Arbitus paused for a moment to watch their reaction, then went on. "Our investigation into both crimes - the shootings today, and the murders of Bobby Coluccio and his children – will continue, and we will expect you to make yourselves available for further questions as they arise. Particularly, you need to tell us immediately if you are contacted by Representative Reese.

"I guess I'd like to add, Mr. Polito, that your little stunt with the limo was not the way we like to see private citizens address such situations."

"I know," Joe said wearily. "It seemed like a good idea at the time. I guess it wasn't too smart."

"That's the way I see it," Arbitus said with a faint smirk. "I hope, if it ever comes up again ... No. I hope it never comes up again."

"Right," Joe said. "But can you tell us something about Pat Sheehan. Is he going to make it?"

Arbitus's face turned serious. He looked down and shook his head. "No. Sheehan died before they could get him into surgery. Apparently his heart just gave out under the strain of the wound."

CHAPTER 34

Arbitus told them reporters would be waiting as they walked out of the station and would probably recognize Joe from his presence at the scene. He suggested Art and Eileen leave first and bring their car around to the side door, where Joe could slip out unnoticed.

It almost worked. Joe was just getting in the Lexus when a young man who had been talking to one of the cops recognized him and yelled, "Hey," and started toward them. Joe ignored him, climbing quickly into the back seat and shutting the door. The reporter watched them drive away, but Joe saw him noting the license number of the SUV.

"Shit," Joe said. "They're going to be all over you, Eileen."

"Why? They don't even know I was there."

"To get to me. They got your license plate. That's all they need to hound you until you give me up. Best thing to do is just give them my name, address and phone number. Maybe that'll be enough to get them to leave you alone."

"Why should you have to take all the questions?"

"Because the more of us they know were there, the more questions we'll all have to face. The less they know, the better."

Eileen invited Art to come out to Lexington, but he just wanted to go home to his own place.

"What about dinner?" she asked. "You want to stop and get something?"

"That's alright," he said. "I'll just walk up to the square and get something at Mike's. I'm kind of looking forward to getting back in the old routine."

Eileen looked at Joe in the rear view mirror. Her eyes were expressionless. "What about money?" she asked Art. "Are you okay?"

"Oh, yeah. I'm fine."

"You know Joe found that wad of hundreds in your apartment. I've still got it, but I think you should put it in the bank. That's a lot of cash to have around."

"I don't want it," Art said.

"Why not?" Joe cut in. "Pat wanted you to have it. There's no strings attached. He didn't expect anything for it."

"I know. He gave it to me to help me hide out. Now I don't have to hide anymore. Maybe I'll give it to the Retreat."

"You can do whatever you want with it," Joe said, "but I don't see any reason why you shouldn't keep it. It was a gift, and it's disrespectful to give away a gift."

"You know I don't mean it that way, Joe," Art said defensively.

"No, but just the same ..." Joe left it at that.

They dropped Art in front of his place on Elston.

"Tell Jake I'll be out again on Wednesday, like always," he said as he got out. "Tell him we're all back to normal, now."

"Okay," Eileen said. "You take care."

Joe got in front and they watched Art trudge up the steps and push aside the warped and scabby front door. When he was inside, Eileen drove slowly down the street.

"Can you come out to Lexington tonight?" she asked, her voice carefully even.

"Sure," Joe said. "I'm not doing anything."

They didn't say much more on the way out to Eileen's house.

Eileen parked in back, and they went in through her private suite. "Make yourself a drink," she said. "I've got to go see how Jake's doing."

Joe went to the liquor cabinet and found the bottle of Blanton's. He poured some into a glass and took it to the sofa, where he sat, staring down on Lexington Common. At one corner of the small park, the Minuteman Statue was softly lit, splitting the sparse traffic that flowed past as if it was protecting the historic green from the onslaught of the modern world. Joe put his drink on the glass-top table and let his head fall back. His limbs felt loose and lifeless. He could not believe it had been only four days since the first time he'd sat with Eileen on that sofa, and now he wondered if this would be the last time. He was too tired to think about it.

"Joe."

Eileen said it softly, but he heard it and opened his eyes. "Huh," he said, surprised out of a sound and dreamless sleep. "I never do that. How long were you gone?"

She was over at the liquor cabinet pouring gin over ice. "About twenty minutes. I wanted to see how he was doing with ... everything he saw."

"How was he?"

She brought her drink over to the sofa and sat down. "He didn't want to talk about it. In fact, he would hardly talk at all. He just sits there, watching TV, but I don't think he's even seeing it."

"It's shock," Joe said. "We're all feeling it. Give it a day or two to wear off."

"I hope so."

They sipped their drinks in silence, looking out at the empty common.

"I can't stop thinking of that old man walking up to that gun," Eileen said, breaking the long silence. "I know he was dying, but ... he volunteered to be shot."

"I've been thinking about that, too," Joe said. "Before the ambulance came, Pat asked me to talk to his wife, tell her why he did it. He seemed to think I'd know."

"Don't you?"

"I know what I think," he said with some irritation.

"What?"

"Loyalty. Pat owed Art – big time. They were friends from school days. Then, Art had to take on the burden of those kids Reese slaughtered, which was the direct result of Pat's mistake. On top of that, Art took the 10 year hitch in Walpole to get Pat off the hook. That's enough for a Somerville guy to take a bullet right there."

Joe drained the rest of his whiskey and went for more.

"You really buy into that old-time code of honor, don't you?" Eileen said while he was still at the liquor cabinet.

He came back to the sofa and sat down. "Not really. That's what led Pat Sheehan to have people killed, probably do it himself, and probably more than once. I don't buy that."

Joe's eyes were wide awake now, and he went on. "But the road he travelled to get from where he was thirty years ago to where he was today – that's something. Maybe it's just because he had so far to go – maybe that's why it's so ... striking."

"What about you, Joe?" she asked. "Where are you on that road?"

He looked at her with a quizzical expression, then laughed. "Me? I'm just your average shithead with a bad temper. If I'm even on that road, I don't know which way I'm going."

It wasn't until later that Joe brought up the subject neither of them wanted to talk about. "I guess we're done looking for Art," he said. "We found him ... or he found us. Anyway, we don't have to look anymore. We can go back to our regular lives."

"What do you mean, 'our regular lives?'?" Eileen asked coldly.

"I mean I can go back to the Town Tavern and read my book, and you can go back to working all the time."

"And just forget about each other? Is that what you mean?"

"No," Joe said carefully. "I'll never forget you."

"But you'd prefer to have me as a memory rather than an actual presence. Is that it?"

"I didn't say that. I just ... You asked me to help you do something, and now it's done. So now we've got to decide what's next."

"I don't see that," Eileen said, struggling to keep her voice steady. Her eyes were bright, but they were framed by an angry frown. "Yes, I'll probably go to work tomorrow, and you'll probably go back to the bar and read, but I don't see any reason why we shouldn't be together tomorrow night."

"I guess I don't either, but I'm still wondering what this is. What's going on with us? What do you want with me?"

"That's not true, Joe. That's not what you're wondering. I've always been clear about what I want from you." She looked him in the eye, but the anger was gone. In its place there was only sadness in her voice and in her eyes. "It's you. You don't know what you want with me."

The minute she said it, he knew she was right, and he was wrong, again. He was lying to her and to himself, and it filled him with frustration. But he couldn't admit it. Instead, he tried an evasion. "Maybe it's just that we're so different."

"We're not so different. You forget, I'm from Somerville, too. I'm Art's daughter, and I lived there until I was 10. Maybe I've spent my whole life trying to get away from it, but I don't think I ever did. That's probably why I love you so much." She got up and blindly went to the window, where she stood with her back to him, facing out, seeing nothing.

"I'm sorry," Joe said. "I guess I'm confused. I ..."

"It's alright," she said softly. "I've never been so sure about anything as I am about you. But I've known all along you didn't feel the same. I can't force you to. I was just hoping you'd come to it on your own. I guess not."

"No. That's not it. I don't know what ..."

"Let's not talk about it now, Joe," she interrupted. "Like you said, we're all a little shook up, tonight. Maybe it will look different in the morning."

Joe slept there that night, but they didn't make love.

CHAPTER 35

The next morning, it didn't look any different, at least not to Joe. It was just as murky and confusing as ever. Eileen did not bring it up – whatever "it" was – and Joe was thankful for that. But it sat between them in the car as Eileen drove Joe home before she went to work, and they both felt awkward trying to talk around it.

There were no reporters waiting on his front steps. Joe kissed her when he got out of the car, but the kiss was more formal than passionate. He asked her to call him when she got off work. Beyond that, they made no plans.

It was a relatively mild morning, with the temperature already climbing past the freezing mark. Joe had had a cup of coffee at Eileen's, but he decided to walk up to the sandwich place and get some breakfast. He wasn't hungry. It was just something to do, and he had a sudden aversion to going up to his empty apartment.

He ordered coffee and a bagel at the counter and took a seat. It was early, and the house copy of the Globe was sitting on one of the tables, more or less intact. Joe picked it up and got a sick feeling when he read one of the headlines below the fold: "Mob Boss Shot, Killed." The secondary headline said: "Off-duty officer also killed in shootout." Despite the misleading headlines, the article was factual as far as it went. Pat Sheehan was identified as "the head of a Somerville criminal gang during the infamous turf wars of the early 80's." Chad Reese was simply "an off-duty Somerville police officer, the son of State Representative Edward Reese of Charlestown," with a one line comment that "police had not been able to locate Representative Reese to notify him of his son's death." The police spokesperson would only say that eyewitnesses had been interviewed and that two other individuals were being sought for questioning. There was no mention of the Coluccio angle, no speculation about the motive for the shootings, but the unstated implication of a police officer being gunned down while protecting the public from an infamous criminal was not discredited. The only hint that there could be another angle to the story was the fact that it contained no words of praise for the fallen officer from his superiors at the Somerville Police Department. For such an article, that was a strange and significant omission, but one that would be noticed by only a few sharp-eyed readers.

Joe immediately thought of Rose and how she would react to the article. Pat must have foreseen the way the shooting would be treated in the news. That was why he asked Joe to talk to Rose - to tell her what really happened. Joe still had no idea what he would say, but he would talk to her as soon as she was ready. He felt he owed Pat that much, and he was enough of an old time Somervillain to consider that sacred.

He walked back to his apartment as the morning rush was piling up on College Ave. When he let himself in, everything was as he had left it the day before, but the place felt alien. He shaved, took a shower, brushed his teeth, and changed his clothes, taking his time at it, but when he finished, it was still only a few minutes past nine. It took a serious effort to concentrate enough to get through another 20 pages of his book.

At 10:00, he called Rose. He wasn't at all certain she would answer. If she had been subjected to the heartless curiosity of the public in the form of prying reporters, he would not blame her for treating the phone as if it was radioactive. He just hoped she would see that the call was from him and remember that he was her friend and might have something to tell her.

"Hello," she said. Her voice was subdued, but not hopeless.

"Hello Rose. This is Joe Polito. I want to tell you how sorry I am."

"Oh, thank you, Joe. I'm so glad you called. Do you know what happened? The police won't tell me very much."

"They're protecting their case, I guess, but yes, I can tell you most of what happened. In fact, that's why I called. After he got shot, Pat asked me to talk to you – if he didn't …"

"You talked to Pat after he got shot?" she said, shocked. "You were there?"

"Yes, I was."

"The police didn't tell me that."

"It seems like they're trying to say as little as possible, but that doesn't mean I have to. I'd like to come over and tell you the whole story, if that would be alright."

"I'd be very grateful. When can you come?"

"Would after lunch be okay? Say 1:00?"

"That would be fine. I've been so … confused. I know Pat hasn't been involved in any kind of criminal activity for quite a few years, but the paper made it sound like …"

"Don't worry. The paper got it all wrong. They just didn't have anything else to print, so they went with old stuff out of the files. I can tell you, Pat didn't die like a criminal. He died more like a hero."

There was silence on the line for a moment. Then Rose took an audible breath. "Thank you, Joe. I never should have doubted that, but it's nice that someone else knows it, too."

"I'll tell you all about it this afternoon, but I don't think it will be long before the truth comes out. Then everyone will know."

"I hope so."

Joe didn't go to the Town Tavern for lunch. He made a tuna fish sandwich and ate it at his kitchen table. He changed into khaki pants and a blue dress shirt with a small check pattern and walked down to the square in time to catch the 12:30 Highland Ave. bus. He got off in front of the high school and walked down the hill. He was 10 minutes early, but he went up onto the wide wrap-around porch and knocked anyway.

Rose greeted him with a wan smile and brought him into the kitchen, where she invited him to sit at a carved oak table. They chatted awkwardly about inconsequential things while she bustled around, making tea for the two of them. Joe could see she was uncharacteristically anxious, apparently hoping her busy hands would occupy her mind and leave no room for painful thoughts and memories. He was relieved when she poured boiling water into a china tea pot and sat down.

She took a deep breath and looked at him with a troubled frown. "It's funny," she said. "I've known this day was coming for quite some time, but when it came like it did, it still took me by surprise. It's hard to believe he's really gone."

"I felt the same way when my parents died," Joe said.

"They must have been young."

"Mid-fifties, both of them, just six months apart."

"Oh my, that must have been hard. Do you have any brothers and sisters?"

"No, just me. What about you? Do you have family nearby?"

"No – a sister in California. We're not close. She didn't approve of Pat."

"Oh."

"She had heard the stories about him, and she wouldn't even meet him. She didn't come to our wedding. It made me very angry with her, and I guess she felt the same about me. Anyway, we exchange Christmas cards now, and that's it."

"That's a shame."

"Yes, it is. She was the big sister, and she always felt she had to protect me, and then I went and ruined all her hopes by marrying a gangster. It was the one and only act of rebellion in my whole life, but I guess it was one too many."

"How did it happen? How did you come to marry a guy like Pat?" Joe asked, with genuine curiosity.

"I guess we must look like an unlikely couple – from the outside," Rose smiled. "But we weren't. I was a sheltered, shy, middle-class girl from Winchester, except that I wasn't a 'girl' anymore. I was 38 years old and I still lived with my parents. I'd hardly ever had a "date." I suppose you would think I was getting a little desperate, but I don't think I was – at least not consciously. I met Pat at a wedding. He was very well-known, and even popular, despite his reputation. I think he had to attend lots of weddings and wakes because of his position. He had people around him most of the time at the reception, and I was mostly standing alone or with my sister and her husband. But, at one point, he happened to be standing beside me and he made some small comment about the wedding. I can't remember what it was, but we started talking, and I found him to be charming – not ignorant or self-important. If anything, he seemed a little unhappy with his public role and glad of the chance to talk to someone who wasn't interested in that. I suppose I was shy and reserved, which was probably different than most of the women he knew. Anyway, he asked me to dance, and he was big and strong and polite and handsome, and I was swept away. Of course, I knew who he was. I'd heard all the stories, too, and I won't say that there wasn't some fascination of the forbidden about him, but I thought it was a harmless thrill, one dance with a dangerous man and a silly school-girl infatuation.

"But then he called a few days later and asked me to go out to dinner with him. That was when my act of rebellion began. Against the wishes of my whole family, I went out with him. We went to a beautiful restaurant on the waterfront in Boston and had a wonderful meal, but the best part is that we took up right where we had left off. He seemed so at ease, and he talked about things that meant something to him. And I surprised myself. I could talk to him the same way. It was a revelation to me, and, I guess, for him too. I think that was when we both knew we were meant to be together."

Rose got up and pulled the basket out of the teapot. She filled two cups and brought out a delicate little pitcher of milk and two teaspoons, placing everything neatly in front of Joe. But she was clearly finding relief in the memories of her courtship, and she went right on telling them to Joe.

"The problem was, this was a man who had been involved in every kind of criminality, including murder. I had no intention of spending my life with someone like that. I couldn't resist going out with

214

him, but I got increasingly despondent about the time I knew I would have to break it off. I was in love with him, but we were too far apart on the most basic issue of morality. It seemed insurmountable.

"I think he must have known how I felt. We never talked about it. It was probably the one thing we couldn't talk about – until, one night, he made his confession. He told me everything he had done. It was a horrible litany of crime and degenerate behavior. I was so horrified, I sobbed through most of it. He said there were reasons for what he did, but he knew they weren't good enough. He was through with that life, ashamed of it, and he promised he'd never go back. Then he asked me to marry him. It was what I wanted more than anything, but I couldn't say yes. I believed everything he said, including his promise to change his life, but it took me some time before I could accept the idea of joining myself to a person who had done what he had.

"Oddly enough, it was my family that finally made me realize what I had to do. Of course, they hated our going out and constantly berated me for it. But the worst time was right after Pat proposed. I hadn't told them about it, but they saw a picture of us in the paper. The paper didn't say anything about Pat's criminal past. In fact, the picture was taken at a charitable event, one of those society page things. But I was smiling up at him, and he was so handsome and confident. Even in the picture you could see that we were in love. My whole family was horrified, mostly because of what their friends and neighbors would say or think. There was a lot of screaming and crying in the house, and they finally told me that, if I wanted to keep living there, I'd have to stop seeing Pat. That's when I knew that, if Pat was really going to change his life, he would be very much alone, and I couldn't let that happen. We would be alone together, and I knew that would be all we'd need to be happy. They made my decision for me, and I never regretted it for one minute."

Rose suddenly fell silent, as if the memories of Pat had become too solid and real to put into words.

"How did he get out?" Joe asked. "I always thought it was almost impossible to get out of the ..." He couldn't think of the right word.

"You mean how did he get out of the gang?"

"Yeah."

"He bought his way out. I think you're right that it was very unusual, but Pat was a very unusual man. He had a reputation for honesty. I know that sounds ridiculous – an honest criminal – but among his gang, and even among his rivals, his word was gold. And you probably also know that the most dishonest and disreputable thing you could do in the old days was to 'rat' on another criminal.

"Before he would set a date for our wedding, he went to his boss - you knew that he put his gang under the control of the New England mob after the gang wars, right? Well, he went to his boss and told him he wanted to step aside. He said his boss was shocked, but it was too big an opportunity to pass up. Most of Pat's ill-gotten fortune was in the form of silent partnerships in legitimate or semi-legitimate businesses. The influence and income potential was very substantial. Pat offered to turn it over to his boss, along with his promise never to breathe a word about the organization's business. All he asked in return was that the boss let him retire peacefully and protect him from any reprisals from elsewhere in the organization. On the value of his holdings and the strength of his word, the deal was struck and Pat was free. Our only regret is that we've had to live on Pat's savings – live quite comfortably, as you can see – but of course those savings came from his years in the gang. We've been the most law-abiding citizens you could ask for since then, but we've lived on that tainted money, and that never felt right."

Rose sighed. "Ah well, it's an imperfect world, and we're not perfect people."

"No," Joe said, "we're not. But there was definitely some good in Pat Sheehan, and I came over today to tell you about it."

Rose nodded. "Yes, you did, and here I've been the one talking all this time. I just wanted you to see Pat the way I do."

"I think I do, and I think it all fits together with what I've learned about him."

Joe told her the story of the Coluccio murders, the banishment of Ed Reese, and the horrible gnawing guilt that finally overcame Art Delaney when Betty Coluccio died. He told her how her husband had helped Art disappear before Reese could shut him up and how he'd gone to sit on Art when he was ready to give up his life to the hit man Reese had hired. Finally, he told her how Pat walked up to Chad Reese and took a bullet so that Art and his family wouldn't have to.

"He didn't have a gun, and he wasn't involved in anything more illegal than trying to keep his friend from being killed. Chad Reese shot him, and then somebody shot Chad, probably somebody from the New England mob. Nobody saw who it was. I was busy getting Art and his family out of there. When I went back, Chad was dead, Ed Reese was gone, and Pat was lying there wounded. But he was still conscious and that's when he asked me to explain it to you, tell you why he did what he did."

"Oh," she exclaimed, as if the words had burned her.

"So, this is what I think. Guys like Pat and Art who grew up in Somerville inherited this strict code of loyalty. It's probably not just Somerville. Something like that code probably exists in lots of places, but it was a big thing while they were growing up. That code was good and bad. It taught them to be generous and take care of their friends and family. On the other hand, it gave them license to kill any one who threatened their small circle. That was the fuel for the gang war. One of the first killings was one of Pat's top guys and one of his best friends. What was he going to do? He knew who was behind it. He couldn't leave it to the cops. He had to avenge his friend, so somebody else had to die, and then somebody else and then on and on until there was nobody left to kill. Looking back, the stupidity of the whole thing is overwhelming. And, facing death, as he was, I think Pat spent a lot of time looking back. It must have brought back all the shame he told you about when he quit the gang.

"Then Art just made it worse. When Betty Coluccio died, it hit him so hard, he started coming apart. And who was the only one he could talk to about it? Pat. Pat must have thought he was soft. Why go to pieces about some poor drunk who froze to death in an abandoned building. But Art's a simple guy. Whatever he's feeling inside, it shows right up in his face. After a while, Pat must have seen the guilt was crushing Art. I think he started to feel it, too. Betty Coluccio and her kids probably looked like the symbol for all his regrets over that bloody gang war, and the whole thing was just as much his fault as it was Art's. That's why he hauled himself back out on the street when he could barely walk, to try and take care of Art as long as he could. He couldn't let Art be the only one to pay for something they'd both been a part of.

"And then there was Chad Reese standing in front of him, waving a gun, ready to kill anyone that threatened him and his father. Guys like Chad were the other main ingredient in the gang war – cold-blooded, remorseless killers. Pat knew them and knew what they could do. He knew Chad could kill all five of us and never lose a minute of sleep about it. There was Art and his daughter, and Art's 10 year-old grandson standing behind him – an innocent kid, just like Bobby Coluccio's son.

"I think that's what was going through his head when he walked up to Chad's gun. That's why he was ready to take a bullet to try to help us get away."

Rose's head was bowed, and she was crying quietly into a tissue. "Oh, Pat," she whispered, "I wish it didn't have to end this way."

"I think it was important to him," Joe said. "It gave him a chance to prove he wasn't the man you read about in the paper."

She looked up at him. "I see what you mean, Joe. I believe that, too."

"I know he had one regret though."

"What?"

"He was sorry not to spend his last few weeks right here with you. That's why he wanted me to tell you why he died the way he did. He didn't want you to think he was ducking that slow death. It was just that he had something more important to do."

"I've been so selfish," Rose cried softly.

"I don't think so, and Pat didn't think so. But I do think he did the right thing – and not just because he saved my life. If he had done anything else, he wouldn't have been the man he wanted to be, or the man you thought he was. In the end, that was more important to him than anything else."

CHAPTER 36

Joe walked home and changed into his jeans and sweatshirt. He grabbed his book and went down to the Town Tavern. It was a little before four and the place was quiet. He got a beer and took it to his table in the back.

A few minutes after five, Tommy Ahearn came into the tavern and rushed over to Joe's table. "Joe," he said breathlessly, "come over to the TV. You gotta see this."

Joe looked up and saw a banner running along the bottom of the TV screen: "Breaking News." He followed Tommy over to the bar and asked Tim to turn it up.

The picture showed a police boat with divers around it pulling a body out of the water near some industrial piers. When the sound came up enough to hear, the newscaster was saying, "... has been positively identified as that of State Representative Ed Reese. Just yesterday, Representative Reese's son, Chad Reese of the Somerville Police, was gunned down in the parking garage of the Museum of Science. Police would not speculate on the cause of the representative's death, but did indicate that the condition of the body suggested that it hit the water with great force. The body was found floating near the mouth of the Little Mystic Channel, which is consistent with a fall from the Tobin Bridge. The time of death was estimated to have been between 1:00 and 3:00 AM last night. Again, a body pulled from Boston Harbor at around 2:30 this afternoon has been positively identified as that of State Representative Ed Reese. A spokesperson for the Boston Police Department will be issuing a statement within the next hour, and we will bring it to you live."

The station cut to a commercial. Tommy got Tim to draw him a beer, and he and Joe went back to the table.

"Wow." Tommy sat down and shook his head. "You believe that, Joe? Ed Reese. Must have been all messed up about his kid, huh?"

"Maybe."

"What else could it be?"

"Maybe somebody threw him off."

"You think so?"

"I don't know," Joe shrugged. "You met his kid, right?"

"I did?"

"Yeah – that guy that came in and talked to you about Art. Right?"

"That was him?"

"Yeah, Chad Reese."

"No shit." Tommy thought back. "I didn't like him."

"Most people didn't. I'm not sure his father liked him enough to jump off the Tobin Bridge for him."

"Hm." Tommy sipped his beer and frowned with concentration, thinking about it. A moment later, he brightened. "Hey Joe, you ever find Art? You were looking for him, for his little girl. Remember?"

"I talked to him yesterday. He wasn't really lost. He just needed some time to think."

"Oh, I know what that's like. I can never find enough time for that."

Joe laughed. "Me either."

A little later, Paul Shea came in. He was in street clothes, and he came right over and sat down with Joe and Tommy. "You heard about Ed Reese?"

"Yeah," Joe nodded toward the TV behind the bar. "It was on the news. What do you hear?"

222

"They got nothing. They're going over video tape of the cars that went through the toll booths on the bridge last night. That's how desperate they are."

"Tommy thinks he might have jumped because of Chad."

Tommy squirmed. "I don't know. It's just a guess."

Shea laughed. "They'd love that. If there was one scrap of evidence that pointed that way, they'd wrap it up like a Christmas present and shove it in the closet. But how'd he get out there? There was no car. Somebody drive him out and say 'Have a nice jump?' You watch, they're going to be asking for tips from the general public. That's when you know they got nothing."

"That's probably how it's going to stay," Joe said.

He was thinking how strange it was to be sitting at his table in the Town Tavern, talking to Paul Shea about a mysterious and violent death, both of them knowing the story behind it, knowing the police knew, and knowing the mystery would probably never be officially solved. The murder/suicide of Ed Reese would join the Coluccio killings and the murder of Chad Reese as open cases. Joe and Paul might be sitting at that table in another 30 years, still knowing the story that linked all those deaths, and still not able to tell it.

"Hey," Tommy said, cutting into Joe's reflections, "the press conference is on."

He got up and moved toward the bar, where a small group had gathered to watch. Paul and Joe got up and followed. The police spokesperson was Boston Chief of Detectives, Daniel Carson. He was standing at a podium, with a background of a blue curtain hung with a large cloth emblem of the Boston Police. He was already into his prepared remarks when Joe and Paul got close enough to hear. As they expected, he wasn't saying much.

"... initial investigations suggest that Representative Reese fell from the Tobin Bridge. Whether he jumped or was thrown is still unknown. Other than the effects of hitting the water with that much force and of being in the water for approximately 12 hours, there are no other obvious injuries apparent, but the coroner has not yet determined the cause of death. We should have the final report within the next few days. In the mean time, our investigations are focused on determining exactly what happened on the bridge. We are asking anyone who crossed the Tobin Bridge between the hours of 12:00 midnight and 4:00 AM, in either direction, to come forward and tell us what they saw – even if you think you saw nothing...."

"That'll be exactly what they saw," Paul whispered to Joe.

When Chief Carson finished his statement, he took questions.

"Was Representative Reese ever contacted with the news of his son's murder?" a reporter asked.

"No," the Chief said, "not by us. Joint efforts of several of the involved police forces were unable to locate him between the time of his son's murder and the time of his own death."

The same reporter had a follow up question. "Do you consider that significant?"

"It's an important aspect of the case that we are actively investigating."

There were a few more questions, but none of them developed much real information. When the news program cut away to the weather, Joe said to Paul, "Come on outside. Let's get some air."

Paul followed him out and they stood on the sidewalk, far enough from the smokers that they would not have to breathe the smoke and could talk privately.

"You're right," Joe said. "They're not going to get anywhere with this, and the real reasons behind it will never come out."

"No." Paul shook his head grimly. "They can't make a case, and they can't release any of that shit. It's just too messy."

"Yeah, messy," Joe said evenly. "But I can't leave it the way it stands, and I want you to help me fix it."

"What are you talking about?"

"You see that article in the Globe this morning about the shootings at the museum?"

"Yeah."

"They made it sound like Pat was the killer and Chad was the heroic police officer protecting the public at the cost of his life."

"I know."

"Well, we've got to fix that."

"What do you mean?"

"We've got to get the truth out."

"How?"

"I think we offer Chief Carson a deal. I can get everyone who was there – Art, me, Eileen, and Jake – we'll all agree not to give interviews about what we saw and what we know if the police release a statement saying that Pat Sheehan was unarmed and protecting innocent bystanders when he was shot by Chad Reese. It's all true, and it lets them avoid a lot of embarrassing questions about the messy truth."

"Jesus, Joe, you got brass balls. You know how much cops like to be pushed around."

"Yeah, I do," Joe grinned. "That's why I want you to be the one to make the offer."

"Why me?"

"I got history with the police. They might not trust me. I just don't want to let that get in the way."

"How'm I going to negotiate with the BPD?" Shea looked pained. "I'm just a street cop."

"You were there for our statements. They know you've been in on this. Just take it up through channels."

Shea stared at him for a moment. "Shit, Joe, I don't know if this'll work."

"I don't either, but it's worth a try. Don't worry. They're not going to shoot the messenger. You know what? Take it through Somerville PD, but call Arbitus at the same time. He'll get it."

Shea said nothing, just continued to stare, with an angry frown.

"But, you know," Joe said, "this has to happen fast. I'm amazed the reporters haven't got to me yet. When they do, I want to know what to tell them. I think the statement should make the late news tonight and tomorrow's Globe."

"You fucking asshole," Shea remarked as he stalked off to his car. But Joe saw him pull out his cell phone to make the call.

Joe walked back into the tavern.

CHAPTER 37

By 7:30, the tavern was filling up. The Bruins were playing Montreal, and the news about the shootings at the Museum of Science and subsequent death of Ed Reese made for lively conversation. Tim was pumping out beer as fast as he could, and Tina was hustling it out to the crowded tables.

Joe's table was no exception. Tommy broke tradition and stayed past his second beer. Al Mathews showed up a few minutes before the Bruins faced off, but he sat with Tommy and Joe. A few minutes later, Joe was mildly surprised to see Lisa Landry come in with Jerry Lyons evidently in tow. Lisa wasn't a regular, and Jerry wasn't much of a lady's man. He was a big awkward Irishman who lived with his mother. Joe waved them over, which got a big smile from Lisa and a somewhat uncertain nod from Jerry. When Art Delaney showed up, they pulled another table together with Joe's to make room.

Tommy was excited to see Art again. He greeted him like a long lost brother. Jerry and Al said it had been awhile, and Lisa gave him a wink and a grin. Art sat down next to Joe and smiled at all the greetings. He looked around the room, with a look of eager interest, taking in the sights and sounds and smells as if they came from someplace new and exotic, rather than the same old place where he'd spent hundreds of nights before.

"So, Art, where you been? We missed you." Tommy said.

"Oh, I had to get some stuff straightened out in my head," Art said, a little embarrassed. "I went to this retreat place in Dorchester. They give you a little room with a cot and you get your meals with the brothers."

"Sounds nice," Tommy said. "Hey, you heard about Pat Sheehan, right? That was too bad, but I guess he was pretty sick, anyway."

"Yeah, it was too bad. He was a good friend," Art said grimly, glancing at Joe.

Joe nodded solemnly.

"What about this shit with Ed Reese and his son?" Al Mathews put in. "What's that all about?"

Lisa had an opinion on that. "I don't know about the father, but the son was a fucking asshole – if you pardon my French. I just met him once, but that was enough. He thought he was hot shit."

Al frowned. "Yeah, but what the hell did the Reese kid have to do with Sheehan? I don't think Pat was going to rob the museum."

Art looked at Joe. "Who knows?"

"The cops aren't saying much," Joe said, "but I heard the kid was a whack job. Maybe Pat was just in the wrong place at the wrong time."

"Maybe," Al said, but he wasn't convinced.

The Bruins played a good game that night. They went down by two goals in the first period, but dominated the rest of the way to cruise to a 7-3 win over their ancient rivals. Jerry and Al went over to the bar to watch the third period, but Lisa didn't mind. A friend of hers named Sandra came over to the table, sat down and started working on the pitchers that Tina kept bringing. She and Lisa launched themselves immediately into a profane and spirited gossip about their mutual friends and enemies. Joe and Tommy and Art watched the game from the table. Since they couldn't hear the TV commentary across the room, they supplied their own. Tommy wasn't normally a big drinker, and the five or six beers he had went to his head, so the commentary turned into a series of wisecracks about the Canadiens' ineptitude. Tommy was laughing his ass off, and Art was adding a little of his own wit. Joe was a bit quieter than usual, but they didn't notice.

The game ended just after 10:00. Al and Jerry came back to the table, but Al didn't sit down. He dropped some bills on the table and pulled on his coat.

"That ought to cover my beer," he said. "I don't know why Tim doesn't set up a barrel in the men's room and start recycling. The stuff doesn't stay inside us long enough to change much. I doubt we'd even notice the difference."

Tommy loved that one. He didn't stop chuckling until Al was out the door. "I got to tell Tim," he said. "He ought to do it, really, just as a joke."

Jerry evidently knew Sandra. He sat down and joined right into the gossip. Tommy started to pour himself another beer, but then thought about it and put the pitcher down.

"Nope. I had too many already. My head feels all wobbly. I'm going home and go to bed." He got up and put on his cap. He dropped a couple of wadded bills on top of Al's contribution. "Sorry, Joe. That's all I got."

"That's fine," Joe said. "Have a good sleep."

Tommy stopped by the bar on his way out and told Al's joke to Tim, who had probably heard a dozen variations before. Tim smiled politely and wished Tommy goodnight. Joe watched Tommy walk out with his usual jaunty step, heading back to his lonely two rooms in the basement, feeling on top of the world.

When Tommy was gone and Joe turned his attention back to the table, he found Art watching him with a faint smile.

"It's a gift," he said.

Joe grinned. "You got that right."

A few minutes later, Eileen walked into the tavern. Some of the crowd had left after the game, but the place still seemed busy and noisy to anyone coming in off the street. She stood just inside the door, looking around.

Joe spotted her immediately. He didn't think he was looking for her, didn't expect her, but the minute she entered the room, he was aware of her. There was no time to think about it, no time to condition his response. He raised his arm and waved her over, with a big stupid smile on his face.

She wore jeans and a black woolen pea coat with a gray patterned scarf wrapped loosely around her neck. Her nose and cheeks were ruddy from the cold night air. She wore no hat and her hair fell thick to her shoulders, shining and dark. This time she wasn't dressed as an alien, but the noise and bustle of the bar seemed to pause as she walked across the room. And this time, there was none of the confident superiority in her bearing. The look on her face was hesitant, almost timid.

"Hi," she said to Joe as she got close to the table.

Art had been listening to Jerry making some point about the Bruins. He didn't notice Eileen until she was at the table. He looked up and surprise flashed across his face that quickly turned to a smile as he looked from her to Joe.

Joe said, "Hi. Have a seat," and he pulled out the chair next to him without getting up. "Jerry, Sandra, Lisa, this is Eileen Merrill, Art's daughter."

"Hi." Eileen smiled at them and unwound the scarf from her neck.

"I didn't know you had a daughter, Art," Jerry said.

"Well," Art said, suddenly serious, "I guess there were a lot of years that Eileen didn't know she had a father."

Lisa had had quite a few beers. They brought a bright and raucous humor to her eyes, and she wasn't about to let the conversation get heavy. "I bet she thought she hit the jackpot when she found out it was you," she said sarcastically.

Eileen took off her coat and draped it on the back of the chair before she sat down. "Now, you be nice to my dad. He always has nice things to say about you."

Lisa grinned proudly. "Yeah? Well, to tell you the truth, I've heard him brag enough about you, I feel like I know you."

"Hey, Tina," Sandra called out, "another glass and another pitcher over here."

"To what do we owe this honor?" Joe asked.

"Well," Eileen sighed, "after Jake went to bed, I figured I had two choices: go through about 50 emails from work or come in here. I decided I'd had enough of work for one day."

"Good choice," Joe said.

"How's Jake doing," Art asked.

"Who's Jake?" Sandra asked from the other end of the table.

Lisa turned to her. "Jake's Art's grandson, and the way he talks about him, you'd think he was a cross between Albert Einstein and Bobby Orr."

"He's okay," Eileen said, answering Art's question, "a little quiet, but he'll bounce back."

Joe was relieved that Tina chose just that moment to bring the pitcher and a fresh glass. She set them in front of him and eyed the bills still sitting on the table with a mock frown. "If that's my tip, Joe, you better take up another collection."

"Tip?" Joe shot back. "You're supposed to tip in dump like this?"

"Oh, yeah. I guess you didn't know, but that's alright. I've been keeping a tab. I think you owe me about $50,000 at this point, and I'd like it by this weekend. I'm planning a trip to Bermuda."

"No problem," Joe said as Tina sauntered off to the next table.

Joe filled the glass for Eileen. "I didn't even think to ask if you wanted something else," he said.

"No, no. Beer's exactly what I want tonight."

At 11:00, the news came on again. Joe stood up.

"I want to go check this out," he said. "Maybe they've got something new on this Reese thing."

Art and Eileen went with him. They grabbed a couple of empty stools at the bar that were close enough to the TV to hear. The first story was a repeat of the news about Ed Reese. There was nothing new, but tacked on at the end, the newscaster added: "In a related development, this evening, police released preliminary findings from their forensic analysis of the shootings yesterday at the Museum of Science. Gunshot residue analysis indicates that Pat Sheehan did not fire a weapon. It also indicates that the bullet that killed him was likely fired by Chad Reese. Police are unaware of any motive for the younger Reese to want to kill Sheehan and speculate that Sheehan may have been attempting to shield someone else from the bullet. Pat Sheehan was in the late stages of terminal cancer and had no more than a few weeks to live."

"Well that's better," Art said as they went back to the table. "At least they didn't call him a dangerous gangster."

"It is better," Joe agreed.

"It's funny, though," Eileen said. "They didn't say anything about the shot that killed Chad Reese."

"I don't think they've got anything on that," Joe said. "And I don't think they're going to get anything, either."

CHAPTER 38

When Joe left the tavern, Eileen and Art left with him. Joe asked Eileen where she'd parked.

"Over on your street," she said. "I thought there might not be any spots in the square."

"Hope you don't get a ticket, but come on, let's walk with Art a ways. I need to talk to both of you."

"What about?" Art asked, as they walked past the dollar store.

"I made a deal with the cops and it looks like they carried through on their end. I told them, if they'd clear Pat's name in all this, we'd keep our mouths shut about the rest. You saw what they put out on the news. I think that's as good as we're going to get. I didn't want to speak for you, but I thought it was a good deal, and it had to get done while it's still on people's minds. Anyway, I can't see the point of putting out the whole story. It raises too many questions – for the cops and for us. What do you think?"

"I agree," Eileen said without hesitation. "I don't see what good we could do by telling it."

They stopped at the corner of Grove Street, and Joe asked, "What about you, Art?"

"It should be alright," he said, somewhat uncertainly. "Holding that story inside for so long almost poisoned me, but now I've told it. I feel like it's out of my system. I don't think I'll ever need to tell it again."

"Good," I'm going to tell the reporters I came along after the shooting and called 911. That'll explain why I was there, and they don't need to know any more than that. If they get ahold of either of you, you don't have to admit you were even there."

"That's fine with me," Eileen said.

"Me too," Art nodded.

Art crossed Grove Street and continued on Elm toward his house, while Joe and Eileen turned toward Joe's. They walked side by side, in silence. When he glanced at her out of the corner of his eye, he saw a peaceful expression on her face that suggested she had nothing more on her mind than the simple enjoyment of a midnight walk in the city. Joe wasn't feeling peaceful. There were things he wanted to say, things they needed to talk about.

But instead he said, "I visited Rose Sheehan this afternoon."

"How is she?"

"She's good, considering," Joe said. "She said she's been facing this day for awhile, but I think it helped that I could tell her how it happened. The cops hadn't told her anything."

"That's rotten."

"Yeah, that's what I thought."

"Is that why you made the deal with the police?"

"Mostly. I would have made the same deal just for Pat, but I don't think it matters when you're dead. It matters to Rose."

"That was nice of you, Joe."

"After what Pat did for us? I'd have to be a real shit not to."

"Well, I didn't think of it, and I bet Art didn't either. And Art was his friend."

Joe didn't say anything. Eileen slid her arm under his, and they walked arm in arm along the shadowy sidewalk.

"Rose is not what you'd expect for the wife of an ex-gangster," Joe said.

"What's she like?"

"Like a sweet old grandmother – except she's not. She and Pat never had any kids. Just the two of them," Joe said, thinking back to the story Rose had told. "The two of them against the world."

"She'll be lonely."

"Yeah."

Again there was silence between them as they turned onto Morrison, but Joe was starting to get comfortable with it.

"You know," he said, breaking the silence and continuing where they'd left off, "the strangest thing about Rose is she's not from Somerville. She came from Winchester, the most proper family you could find. They pretty much disowned her when she married Pat."

"Really?"

"Yeah, but she got Pat to quit the gang business. They both gave up a lot to be together."

Eileen thought about it for a few steps. "I'll bet they didn't feel like they were giving up much at all," she said softly, but with some conviction.

"Maybe not. Rose seems to miss her family, but she said she didn't regret it. And Pat apparently volunteered to give up all the money and power he had in the gang. It sounded like it was something he wanted to do anyway."

"And they got each other," Eileen said. They stopped in front of Joe's place, and she pointed across the street. "There's my car over there."

Joe took a few steps toward the Lexus and examined the windshield. "Good," he said, "no ticket. Come on up, I'll get you my visitor pass."

"Oh," she said, "I'm staying?"

Joe looked stricken. "Uh, yeah," he said. "I hope so. I mean, can you?"

"I guess so," Eileen laughed, "if you insist."

Joe grabbed her hand and pulled her up the steps. "I do," he said.